to:

from:

# Merry Fucking Christmas

by Joe Movick

# Merry Fucking Christmas

ISBN: 978-1-7360980-0-4

Cover art by Xavier Comas
Edited by Brooks Becker
Interior Calligraphy by Jess Deugan

For all inquiries:
mfc@bishopspub.com

First Edition

*To all whom Christmas is . . . complicated.*

# CONTENTS

# Black Friday

Helen looked out across the sea of children. Thirty, maybe forty brats and their parents on the knife's edge between an anxious queue and an unholy riot.

Black Friday.

The inaugural gathering of children waiting to sit on Santa at the mall. Why a couple hundred people a day would wait an hour and pay forty bucks just so their kids could sit on a stranger's lap baffled Helen. Whatever their motivation, a raise from last year to more than minimum wage and a month straight of work was worth anything the heathens could throw at her.

Nagging at the back of Helen's brain wasn't the fact that she had an entire month of this mess ahead of her, but that she was entering year five of the routine. Five years of the food court. Five years of watching the haggard old lady who worked at the popcorn kiosk. Five years since she had the big "revelation" and started down her dream path. Yet here she was.

A cheap apartment with one toothbrush. An agent who kept telling her, "Someday really soon." And the only consistent thing in her life was a mall gig. Helen and Santa versus the worst that the suburbs could throw at them.

Santa was Doug this year. Doug was a balding thirty-year-old first timer. A decade or so of moderate substance abuse and, likely, accompanying diet; Doug had aged enough to pull off the Santa look. Tired, red-shot eyes and a smoker's rasp complemented his rotund midsection. The only accessory he needed was the fake white beard.

Helen pitied Doug for his sake, but she was disgusted by him for her own sake. Surely he had done something wrong to be working this job in his thirties. She would not become Doug.

Doug was yelling Helen's name. An autistic kid on his lap was trying to give Santa a titty-twister. Doug let out a yelp and a muffled curse word. A young mom at the front of the line wearing a "It's the most fun-derful time of the year" sweater scowled at him.

Helen grabbed the kid from Doug and set him down by his parents. The parents simply laughed an unconvincing "sorry" and asked the kid if he enjoyed talking to Santa.

"Titty-twisty!" was all he replied.

Helen laughed.

"Thanks for rushing over," Doug snapped.

"You're fine," Helen said. "Santa doesn't have nipples."

Doug huffed, "When I call your name, I need you to drop everything and come help me. I'm vulnerable up here."

Helen opened her mouth to summon a sarcastic retort. She didn't work for him. She wanted to tell him to *pretend* to be a jolly old man. She wanted to tell him to get bent. Instead she slumped and walked to the front of the line to retrieve the next spoiled child and accompanying uptight mom.

Doug called after her, "I need a break."

"Be patient, Doug," Helen said under her breath as she walked the next kid and the mom with the sweater up to Santa. The mom may have actually hissed at her.

"Don't make me wait long," Doug said.

"Okay, okay," Helen said. "Santa, this is…" she began.

The hissing, fun-derful mom perked up and shuffled an additional two children towards Helen.

"This is Jonah, Ruth, and Abraham!"

Three five-year-olds bumrushed Doug, nearly knocking him out of his ornamental chair.

"Triplets?" Helen asked the mother.

"My prides and joys." The mother beamed.

Helen made her way further into the crowd of people, leaving Doug by himself with the "threefer," as she labeled any sit-down where Santa had to endure more kids than he had knees.

"Attention, North Pole guests! Thank you so much for coming to see Santa! After Shadrach, Meshach and Abednego are finished up, we will be taking a short five-minute break," Helen called out, doing her best to ignore the looks of reproach from the mothers, fathers, and children in front of her.

*Santa needs his pot break, and if I wasn't so afraid of hearing him talk about his life choices I'd probably join him,* Helen thought.

A minute later, the triplets ran to the photo counter with their mother and Santa ran outside for a smoke. Helen offered a parting smile to the crowd of people and stepped behind the wooden sleigh, where she could be just out of eyesight from the line.

She pulled her phone out to open a dead conversation with "Jim."

Jim had *hit it and quit it* with Helen last week. Helen wasn't dating for a husband . . . she also wasn't casually sleeping around with anyone who had the mental fortitude to swipe their fingers to the right.

Jim was. His profile photo was from twenty-five, and he'd said it was recent. The Nickelback T-shirt suggested otherwise. Helen casually ignored both red flags.

Her standards habitually dropped around the holidays. Something about the lonely apartment and the single toothbrush by her sink contrasted with the season's deluge of advertisements promising joy, merriment, and family gatherings.

Jim had walked into the bar looking thirty-five. Two drinks, something about meeting Helen's cat, the drive to her apartment and five pantless minutes later, he was gone.

Helen had three, "Hey! How are you?" messages (one every other day) out to Jim since their tussle in her sheets. Nothing back.

Douche.

Her therapist had convinced Helen to forget about it, but an ominous itch this morning had rekindled her anger at the old man. The itch went away, but the message was getting longer and snarkier every time Helen opened her phone.

Whether she'd be bold enough to send it, Helen didn't know, but writing it felt therapeutic.

"It's been five minutes!" a dad called from the line, pointing to a stopwatch app on his phone.

Helen straightened herself up and knocked on the window outside to signal Santa. She returned to her post and called to the waiting families, "Thank you so much for your patience! This is a very busy time of the year for Santa."

"What is he, on a conference call with the reindeer?" the same dad asked out loud. There was peppered laughter from the crowd.

They were growing hostile. Helen did not want a repeat of 2018.

Then she saw the face that went with the voice . . . and like a bad movie of the week, it couldn't have been anyone else. It was him.

Jim.

And he was standing with two kids. They looked ten and eight. Boys. Maybe it was the lighting, or the two grown children, but suddenly he looked not a day under forty. And kids??

Her face grew red. Several adults in the crowd shied looks at her. Then Doug came back inside the North Pole, and the kids all cheered.

"Helen?" Doug said after a few moments, motioning to the line of waiting customers.

"Oh," she grunted, and came back to her senses. "Okay everyone, Santa is back. Who is our next special guest?"

She mindlessly went back to her job. Autopilot. But her gaze never fully left the douchebag. She cycled kids through the line, onto the big red lap, and out to the pay station.

And she watched.

And he was nearing the front of the line.

"Ouch!" Doug called from behind her.

A kindergartner with reindeer antlers was kicking him in the shins.

"Thank you, thank you," Helen mimed as she hustled the kid and his parents to the photo counter.

Maybe she could confront Jim in front of his kids. And in front of the crowd. Surely he must have recognized her. How could he not? Was she just one of a long list of hookups to him?

One more kid to go, and Jim would be in the front of the line. Helen's heart raced. Did she have the guts to do it?

Wouldn't she be working on a hit Netflix show right now instead of inside this god-forsaken mall if she'd learned the art of confrontation? Would she ever change? Wasn't this her chance?

She watched Jim get down on a knee and straighten his younger son's hair. He licked his finger and wiped some ice-cream from the kid's chin.

It seemed like the little kid really loved his dad. The older one too. They were so excited to be here with him. Whatever else was going on in their lives, these two kids were happy right now.

It reminded Helen that this awful job did have a silver lining. And for the first time in her mall elf career, Helen saw a small glimpse of humanity in this cesspool of holiday depravity.

*Well . . .* Her inner copout was speaking up.

Maybe he was a good dad. He wasn't a complete asshole on the date, even for a one-night stand. Maybe he just had some steam to blow off.

It would be nice to have someone around this Christmas.

Even him.

He probably just lost her number.

"Oh my god, I almost missed it!" a woman called behind Jim.

This tall, beautiful woman ran to him and gave him a kiss. She kissed both of the boys as well. She had a nice big rock on her left hand. And him. Jim. Now that he was standing closer to her, Helen could see that he had a gold wedding band on.

"Fuck. Ing. Ass. Hole," Helen whispered.

Her mind raced through that night again . . . for the thousandth or so time. No wedding band. No mention of kids. No mention of wife. No chance they were going back to his place. He was out of her apartment before the evening news came on.

He'd used her goddamn toothbrush and left it lying in the bottom of the sink . . . the bristles resting on the oxidized drain hole.

" . . . Miss! Hello?" Helen heard, and she came back to.

"Sorry," Helen said, scanning the crowd.

The wife. With the big rock. "Santa looks like he's ready for our kids now?"

Helen spun to Doug.

"Of course!" she said. "This way, please."

As Helen turned her back, Jim whispered to his wife, "Not the best and brightest working at the North Pole today." His wife laughed and shushed him.

After she helped the kids onto Santa's lap, Helen turned to the husband and wife standing on the side of the stage.

"You look really familiar," Helen told Jim. And swung her eyes from him to his wife. She blinked them open a bit further just to show off their bright green hue and tilted her hat to the side.

*Yes, I'm dressed like a cheap fucking elf, but I* am *attractive, and your husband* does *know me*, was the message.

21

"Sorry, I doubt it," he responded, nervously pulling his phone out.

Helen saw the recognition and regret in his eyes. It seemed like an appropriate payback. No big scene. No nasty words. Surely this could turn into a fight for their car ride home and, god willing, go on for another couple days.

Helen turned back towards the kids but watched the ground, listening for a quiet argument. She heard the wife nudge her husband. "How do you know that kid?"

"Not right now," he said.

"Jim . . ." she started.

And then it happened.

"It's my turn!" One of the kids on Santa's lap yelled.

Helen looked up.

"No!" the younger one yelled back. "You're taking too much time! I didn't get to ask for anything!"

"Kids . . ." Jim started, but his voice cut out just as the younger boy threw a haymaker at the elder. The punch didn't land, but it began a frenzy of fists, head-butts, and kicks.

Doug dodged the first couple volleys, then the older kid swung a little too wide and caught Doug right in the eye socket. Defensively, he stood up and both kids fell to the stage floor. Someone in the crowd gasped.

Well . . . let's be honest, several people in the crowd gasped as Santa dumped the two children off his lap.

"Oh my god," the mom yelled. She and Jim ran to their children, who were still fighting. The younger brother had engaged the elder in a headlock.

Jim strode right past his kids, dug his heels in, and shoved poor Doug-Santa off the stage and onto the tiled floor. Doug was so stoned, he didn't catch himself and smacked his head on the tiles.

He lay dead still.

Then more of the crowd yelled and gasped and protested and mumbled and judged and sipped their peppermint lattes and tweeted and judged some more.

Helen screamed, "Doug!"

The two kids were still fighting, and their parents had to struggle to separate them.

"Jim!" the wife yelled. "You could have killed him."

Helen was kneeling next to Doug. He *wasn't* dead, thank god. He *was* mumbling and talking gibberish. Who knew if it was the fall or the marijuana.

"You ok?" she asked Doug over and over again.

He opened glossy eyes and managed a nod of the head. A man ran over saying something about "help" and "doctor." Helen figured that was good enough, and she stormed over to the family, her silly hat falling off. Her emerald eyes grew fierce.

"Someone call the cops on this asshole!" Helen pointed at Jim.

"That seems a little extreme," Jim's wife said.

"I barely pushed him," Jim added.

Helen walked to within a foot of Jim, the fire in her eyes raging. She didn't have a plan, only anger, and being this close . . . smelling his expensive, stinky cologne again . . . the sloppy sex, the rushed departure, the no calling, the kids, the wife.

And now, the violence.

A sudden rage came out of Helen. She swung an open hand at the tall, dark, attractive jerk's stupid, dumb, symmetrical face.

"What are you doing?" Jim yelled, easily dodging the swing.

She staggered, trying to regain her balance.

"Jim, how do you know this girl?" the wife was pleading.

"I don't know her honey, jesus," he responded.

Helen laughed and shook her head, "You are such an asshole."

"How do you know my husband?" the wife asked Helen, her tone venturing on apocalyptic.

The next word out of Helen's mouth was going to feel like justice.

"Tinder," she said.

Jim slunk.

Helen continued, "He said he was twenty-five, feeling singly and mingly and didn't mention anything about his *wonderful* family."

"Come on," Jim protested.

"We went out for drinks, back to my place for five minutes of what may technically or, I guess, biologically speaking, meet the definition of sex, and then he must have rushed home to you."

Jim's wife made a strange sound. Then coughed, then made the sound again. And again and again, the more she did it, the more it started to sound like a chuckle.

She couldn't help herself, she started laughing out loud. And it grew louder until Helen was the one who felt uncomfortable.

"I knew it!" the wife said at last. "I FUCKING knew it. Your stupid guys' nights out. You don't have any guys! I knew it, but it's so good to hear out loud."

"Honey," Jim pleaded, "I don't know what she's talking about."

"Save it," she said back.

"I would never hurt you, I promise," Jim said. "You are everything to me. I've never been with anyone else."

"Well, I have," she stopped him.

"What?"

"The neighbors." She smiled at him.

"The who? What?! Which neighbor?"

"Starting in the summer when you skipped coming home twice in one week. I thought to myself, this has been one-sided long enough."

"Why are you saying neighbors, plural?" Jim asked.

"And after that one I thought, hey, that was fun. Let's do it again. And again. And again," his wife continued.

. . . and Helen decided her role in the conversation was over.

Maybe it was the end of the chaos or the threat of police, but the North Pole was nearly empty. Probably to Starbucks for a debrief. Only the unhappy family, Helen, Doug, and the doctor dude were left in the open space.

As Helen tiptoed over to Doug, she couldn't help but overhear several of the most bland, white, suburban dad names imaginable coming from Jim's wife. "Joe, Bob, Chuck . . ."

*Get' em, girl.*

She knelt next to Doug. He was seated on the floor, propped up against a candy cane. Helen asked the doctor guy what he thought.

"Concussion," he said. "Definitely. But otherwise he seems just fine. I'd say he needs someone to watch him for the rest of the evening. Are you his girlfriend?"

"Hell no," Helen said.

"Well, I can't in good conscience leave him here all by himself," the man frowned.

Doug sighed and looked at his shoes with the pity only a lost puppy or a true-to-god loser could conjure.

And Helen realized two things. One, she didn't have anyone either. An embarrassing truth, sure, but one that was healthy to admit. Two, that this chapter of her month would bookend in another random guy staying over at her apartment. On the couch. Doug was definitely staying on the couch.

And she was going to hide her fucking toothbrush.

# To Gift a Puppy

Honey?" Nick asked, tapping on the open door to his bedroom. He'd given his daughter the room and taken the couch Christmas Eve.

"Yeah?" Holly replied.

She sat on the bed scrolling through her phone. Fourteen, she probably couldn't help the apathetic roll of her eyes.

"I'm not sure what tradition has been for you the last couple years," he said, "but I thought we could open one of your presents tonight, just like we used to."

"When?" she asked.

This would get harder every year. Holly would grow to look more and more like her mother, while her mother would continue to find new ways to undermine Nick, the cycle continuing until Holly turned eighteen and left for Rio, or Canada, or any distant corner of the world they'd both be too broke to visit.

"Well, if you're busy . . . " he paused.

Holly glanced up from the phone for the first time. "What is it?" she asked, more eager now.

"What is what? Your present?"

"Yeah."

"I'm not going to tell you, you'll just have to open it."

"Now?" she asked.

"Of course."

She powered down the screen on her phone and sat up. "Now is great!" She hopped off the bed and skipped out of the room.

Nick waited for her to turn the corner and then walked out to the hallway closet.

Twenty minutes ago a shady friend of a friend had quietly dropped off a gift-wrapped $12 mixed-breed that Nick had placed it in the closet. Nick always appreciated a good deal and figured, worst case, he was saving this thing from a bad home.

"Dad! Hurry!" Holly called from the living room.

The box in the closet wiggled and made a quiet yelp.

"Shh," he whispered. Nick picked up the present. He walked with a little jig in his step to the living room with the gift.

Holly sat on the far side of the couch. Phone back up. She'd picked out a present and set it on the couch next to her.

She was in her uniform. White Converse, tight jeans, and a used-to-be-bright-red Ohio State hoodie. She was already almost as tall as her mother, which put her a good inch or two taller than Nick.

"I thought this one looked good," she said without looking up.

He pictured her, not fourteen, but four. She was so excited the night before Christmas that she'd refused to get up from the couch.

She wanted to see Santa. Holly's mom, Midge, finally gave up trying to talk her out of it and went to bed. Nick fetched Holly's pony pillow, curled up next to her, and they fell asleep together on the couch until Christmas morning. The next year it was the same thing and the year after that, and it kind of became tradition. A tradition that made putting presents under the tree inconvenient but became Nick's emotional anchor for the holiday.

And here she was, back on the couch. Of course, this couch was different. Craigslist. There was no tree in this sad little apartment, and Midge had only lent Nick their daughter for Christmas Eve because she was working night shift at the hospital. But still, the nostalgia of it all . . .

The box Nick held let out a small yelp. Holly dropped her phone. She looked at her dad with ginormous eyes.

"Dad . . . did that box . . ."

The gift yelped again.

"Oh my god. I mean. Gosh." Holly beamed. "Dad!"

She jumped to her feet and gave her dad a huge bear hug made somewhat awkward by the box he was holding. Still, it was the first authentic contact they'd had in . . . in a long time.

"Is he for here? Or for mom's? Or can I just have him always?" Holly danced on her toes. Her eyes sparkled.

The gift yelped, barked, and bounced around in Nick's arms.

"We'll have to see what your mom thinks about having a dog at her house, but as far as I'm concerned, *she* is yours. Wherever you want to keep her," he said.

As he spoke, Nick cringed. He'd balanced life on the high-road of divorced parenting for two years. This moment was his freefall.

Holly gave him a kiss.

31

"Mom'll have to let me, or I'll just threaten to move in with you."

"We'll talk about that later. Go ahead and open it," he told his daughter, setting down the shaking gift.

Holly carefully removed the top of the box. She gave another big smile, and out jumped a brown mutt.

The dog was bigger than Nick had expected. Longer and taller, but skinny, very skinny. She had shaggy, somewhat-groomed hair, two giant brown eyes, and an ear-to-ear smile locked on her face.

Holly reached for it, but the dog scampered back from her.

"Go ahead, honey," Nick said "I'm sure she's just a little shaken up. Show her some love."

Holly reached for the dog again. Nick saw the smile grow even wider on its face.

*Weird.*

"I don't know, Dad," Holly said as she took an instinctive step back towards the couch.

Determined to make the moment a special memory, Nick lunged after the dog and grabbed it.

The dog thrashed its head back and forth, the smile opening to a multitude of gnashing teeth looking for a part of Nick to latch on to. Holly dodged clouds of white foam flying from the dog's mouth as its head swung from side to side.

Nick still thought the dog was acting in a funny, albeit benevolent way and decided to set it down so it could run to Holly and give her a big kiss. It seemed to really want to. He set the dog onto the rug and smiled at his daughter as the creature set off in a sprint towards her.

"NO!" Holly screamed, and jumped up onto the couch. She swung a throw pillow at the dog. It side-stepped her and ran into the kitchen.

"What are you doing Holly?" Nick demanded.

"Dad!" she replied, "Look at it!"

Her trembling finger pointed to the kitchen doorway. At the threshold the dog stood, panting, smiling, drooling. Looking longingly at its new family. Nick frowned. He looked back at his daughter. She'd resumed crying.

He didn't get it.

Why did everything he try turn to shit? Nick wondered if Holly was more of a cat person, or maybe if she just felt more comfortable around purebreds. He shook his head, trying to clear his thoughts.

"Stop living in the fantasy of what you want things to look like, and start living in the reality of where they are." Nick could hear his good-for-nothing ex–marriage counselor saying.

He tried. Focus. Reality.

The dog was in the kitchen staring at him. The smile on its face showed gnarly, sharp teeth. They were dripping with white foam. Its head was tilted to one side, almost as if it was asking a question. The longing in its eyes was different too. It wasn't looking for a family to love, it was longing for a family to bite.

Nick screamed.

The dog started barking at him. Nick had made himself a target.

"Dad! Stop!" Holly pleaded. "Call the police."

"They turned my phone off."

"What?"

"You call them, use your cell phone!" Nick pleaded.

Holly looked for her phone. It lay on the floor just a few feet from the demon animal.

Nick shook his head at her, "Wait . . ." he started, but Holly was already off the couch.

The dog's left eyebrow raised as it watched Holly approach. It shifted its weight onto its back paws and somehow in its damaged brain calculated an intercepting angle on her. Nick cried out and started to run towards the both of them, everyone converging on a single point in empty space.

Holly and the dog got there first. Nick watched in horror as it chomped down on her outstretched arm.

Holly shrieked in pain. The dog was now attached to her arm. It flung its body this way and that sinking its teeth further into her forearm. Low budget horror movie streams of blood sprayed all around the room.

Nick grabbed the dog's enormous head and tried to pry it off of his daughter's arm. When he pulled, the dog would simply bite deeper and gnash its teeth further into the tender insides of Holly's flesh. Nick drew back and punched the dog in the nose, but he only hurt his hand.

He thought of the revolver under his mattress and the bullets in the . . . pantry? Hallway closet?

Did he have bullets for that thing?

Didn't he bet *and* lose the gun in that poker game?

Then another thought. The apartment came furnished with a wood-burning fireplace. As Nick looked around the room desperate for help, he saw it: a poker, hung with the other tools just a few steps out of reach. Holly's eyes pleaded with him.

Nick grabbed the poker, swung it at the dog, and sunk it into the beast's hind leg. The dog made a deep, low grunt and let go of Holly's arm. It threw Nick a look of pure evil and ran into the bedroom, leaving behind a trail of blood equal parts Holly's and its own.

Holly collapsed into her dad's arms.

---

Nick pulled into the emergency circle at the hospital. He was yelling out of his car window at a police officer on the curb. Apparently the circle was only for ambulances. They'd have to park and walk through the main entrance, passengers near death or not. Nick gave in, compromising for a stolen handicap spot near the front entrance.

What followed, once inside the hospital, was a major letdown considering all the medical television Nick had watched. Most Americans, when finally presented with an actual medical emergency, think the back pay of all their insurance premiums will coalesce into a heroic, dramatic miracle of science.

Instead, they were told to sit with the other twenty or so people in the waiting room. The nurse at the front desk glared at the blood Holly'd dripped onto the floor in the lobby on her way in. He tossed a rag at Nick and told him to put pressure on his daughter's wound.

"We need to see someone right now," Nick said, motioning to the room full of people. "My daughter is bleeding."

"Bro," the man said, "genius is patience, Isaac Newton."

Nick already regretted the next thing coming out of his mouth, "Midg-- Margaret Snow-- Allen, it's Margaret Allen now. She's a nurse here."

*Woof.*

"And?"

"This is her daughter. I think she'd want us to be taken care of?" Nick tried and failed to sound entitled.

"Here's some paperwork, go take a seat."

It was all a far cry from Holly being rushed in on a stretcher, doctors yelling out complex medical terms while George Clooney straddled the stretcher and applied pressure on the bite with his bare hands, sweating, swearing, everyone pulling out the stops— breaking all the rules—to save her life.

Instead, quietly, they sat in a huge waiting room full of strange people. It wasn't *ER*, it was the DMV.

Holly's arm was awkwardly wrapped in the towel they'd been given. Nick hoped her constant shaking was shock and not blood loss.

He was afraid. Afraid for his daughter's health. Afraid of what the doctor might say. Afraid they may never see a doctor. But one fear loomed greater and more immediate. The knowledge that Holly's mother was somewhere in the very same building, and that she would eventually find out they were here.

One emergency room visit wouldn't be enough to justify a new custody hearing, but the wrath of his ex-wife would be far worse than that of any court. He'd gladly put himself on trial in Nuremberg before he'd sit and have coffee with that woman.

He deeply regretted dropping her name at the front desk.

"Snow? Holly?" a nurse called out finally, her head peeking through the swinging doors.

"Yes, here!" Nick yelled.

---

"Merry Christmas," Nick said, motioning to the clock on the wall. Its hands crossed midnight just as Holly woke from a short power nap.

It was the tail end of their third hour in the ER. Holly was on an IV and her arm had finally been cleaned and bandaged with something other than a janitorial rag.

"What did the doctor say?" Holly asked.

"Still hasn't been in, honey," Nick replied. "How do you feel?"

Holly made an exaggerated, prehistoric "ugh" sound.

Nick glanced down at her bandaged arm. Every time he did, an involuntary shudder would shoot through his body. The thought of those dozen or so jagged teeth writhing and gnashing between the two bones in her forearm made him queasy.

The intercom in the hallway blurted some code words, and several staff rushed past their room. Another customer butting in front of them in the queue. Nick looked at his daughter. He could see pain in her eyes. Some fear too. He kept himself from asking her how she felt every twenty seconds, even though it was all he could think of.

"Mom?" Holly asked.

"Haven't seen her either."

"Okay."

Nick didn't want to defend his ex-wife, but he did try to think of an explanation for her absence that would put Holly more at ease. Three hours since Nick blurted his ex-wife's name to the man at the front desk. He thought name-dropping the head nurse at the hospital's NICU would speed things up for them.

It hadn't.

"I'm sure she's really busy," Nick offered.

"Sure," Holly said.

"How are things at home?"

"Fine?" Holly answered, sounding unsure.

"Are you guys getting along alright?" he asked.

A minute or so passed without an answer.

Nick watched a reporter on the muted TV in the corner interview a volunteer at the animal shelter. She held a dog very similar to the demon creature still wreaking havoc in Nick's apartment.

"Maybe I should call in and warn them?" he joked.

"I think Mom doesn't ever want to yell at me because she's afraid I will take sides with you the moment she disciplines me," Holly said. "So she just redirects all her anger and frustration to complaining about you. Your laziness, your lack of direction in life, bad eating habits, bla, bla, bla."

Nick nodded. Smart kid.

"But really," she continued, "those are all things she's mad at me about. I mean, I'm not perfect, and maybe she thinks I'm more like you than I am like her, but it's not like I'm a bad person."

"I think she's trying . . ." Nick started.

"I mean . . . I *am* half you," Holly said. "I understand that you're sometimes lazy and your brain doesn't work as fast as hers does, but get over it, woman. She's not perfect either. I mean it's not like she was home much before the divorce, and she still barely spends any time with me."

Nick took a deep breath in.

"I'm sorry to vent. It's just that none of my friends really understand," Holly finished.

"We've put a lot of pressure on you during the divorce. We probably still are." Nick turned the TV off and moved closer to Holly.

"The thing about your mother . . ." he began.

Then the door to their room burst open and Nick almost physically swallowed his tongue.

His ex-wife, Midge, stormed into their hospital room. She ran to the bed and gave her daughter a huge hug.

"Oh my god, honey, are you OK? I can't believe what happened to you. Did they administer anesthetic? Did they give you a rabies vaccine yet? How about the RIG? Who is seeing you?"

She diverted her attention to Nick "How could you? Why wouldn't you call me? I've been here without a clue! Where do you get off?"

And back to Holly. "I'm so sorry, honey. What do you need? Water? Food? Where is the doctor?"

"That's the question of the day," Nick sighed.

"You . . ." Midge turned to him. "Why on god's great earth would you not call me?? You've been here for how many hours!?"

"Mom!" Holly interrupted. "I'm fine. Dad told the guy at the front desk to tell you we were here."

It wasn't the truth, but it wasn't *too* far from it. Nick kept silent.

"Where were you? What kind of dog bit you? Was it one of your dad's parties?" Midge asked.

"No, Mom. It was my Christmas present," Holly said.

"Oh . . . Christmas present! Wow, Nick," Midge snapped.

This was already the longest Nick had been in a room with the woman since moving his few possessions out of the house after they'd split. He looked from her to his daughter and back. The two tall, dark-haired, insistent women.

"Midge," Nick said. "I'm sorry they didn't tell you we were here."

He could tell Midge had kept up with her anger management classes, given that her fingers were waving wildly around the room rather than clenched around his neck.

Midge sat on the other side of the bed and held Holly's hand. Nick took pleasure in the fact that, for a brief moment, Holly seemed more emotionally distant from her mom than her dad.

"I dropped your name at the front desk. That dude up there is something special," he said.

"Can you explain what happened?" she asked, nostrils flared but voice guardedly calm.

"Yes, I can actually, and it's not that big of a deal," Nick offered. "Remember how we used to give Holly a present on Christmas Eve?"

Then the damn door to their room swung open again. A small, stocky woman walked in like she owned the entire hospital.

"Hello. I'm Dr. Bahadi. I do apologize for the wait, it has been a busy night," the woman said, acknowledging Nick, Holly, and Midge.

Dr. Bahadi walked over to Holly and butted Nick out of his spot.

"How are you feeling, honey?" the doctor asked as she lifted Holly's arm up.

"Fine," Holly answered, "maybe a little tired . . "

"Does this hurt?" the doctor asked, moving Holly's arm around in a semi-circle.

"No."

Midge leaned forward. "Hello?" she said with expectant eyes.

"Hello," the doctor replied, drily. "Now Holly. Can you flex your fingers back and forth for me?"

Holly did as the doctor asked.

"Any pain?" Dr. Bahadi questioned.

"No," Holly said.

Nick could feel the temperature in the room rising.

"How about here? Any pain?" the doctor asked Holly, pointing to her elbow.

"Did you just start here recently?" Midge interrupted.

"No, ma'am," Dr. Bahadi answered. "How long ago was it that you were bitten, Holly?"

"I'd say," Holly started, pretending her mom wasn't about to breathe fire into the room, "around seven o-clock? So maybe five hours ago?"

"Good news is, you are going to be fine. I've had patients who've waited much longer than you before being treated and they've all had full recoveries," Dr. Bahadi said. She referenced Holly's clipboard. "It's going to be a lot of shots over the next several weeks, but then you'll be back to normal. You're not pregnant, are you?"

Holly blushed.

"Of course not!" Midge answered. "How could you . . ."

"It's ridiculous to think . . ." Nick started.

"Please, Mom, Dad," Dr. Bahadi said to them, keeping her attention on Holly. "I could ask your parents to step out for a minute if you'd like."

Midge's face glowed the red hue of smelted iron ore.

Nick's gut reaction was to go to her and stop her from murdering the poor doctor, but he realized that her behavior was no longer his responsibility. He literally paid her money every month to stay out of her business.

Midge stood up. "I will not be leaving the room. Holly, tell this woman you're not pregnant."

"Ma'am . . ." Dr. Bahadi started.

"Don't you *ma'am* me, missy!" Midge fumed. "I have been working at this hospital for over ten years and I've never heard of you! Whatever you're doing right now, it is not caring for my daughter!"

"Ma'am," Dr. Bahadi said again. Calm.

"She is not fucking pregnant!" Midge yelled. "She's fourteen!"

"Mi--" Nick got half of a syllable out before the death stare passed over him. His voice stopped, turned, and retreated back into his throat, the sound reabsorbing into his vocal cords.

Holly sank further down into the hospital bed. Her face redder than her mother's. Nick wished he could do something, but he knew he was the lowest-ranking person in the room. He was so low on the totem pole that he'd likely have to ask the fake shrub in the corner of the room for permission before he spoke.

Midge was still standing over the bed and had begun to shake her finger at Dr. Bahadi. "Grab that phone and call a real doctor in here. I know Dr. Smith is on site. I just saw him an hour ago!"

The doctor did pick up the phone. She spoke into the receiver with that same stern, yet blasé voice. "Yes, room 2113. I'm going to need . . ."

Another voice interrupted her from the intercom in the hallway. "Code blue. Room 2110. Code blue."

The doctor hung up the phone, forgetting any of them existed, and ran out of the room.

Nick and Holly turned to Midge, looking for some kind of explanation for the last several minutes.

"That woman is not coming back in here," Midge said.

"You didn't have to be so mean to her, Mom," Holly offered.

"Yes, honey. Yes, I did," Midge said, matter of fact. "This is a place of medicine, and you always have to speak to your needs or you'll get steam-rolled. Healthcare workers do our best, but we don't know when enough is enough sometimes and . . ."

Then Midge's pager buzzed on her hip. She glanced at it and gave a look of defeat. "Shit."

"Mom?" Holly asked.

"It's alright," Midge said. Her demeanor instantly changed, as had the doctor's. "I have to go. I'm so sorry, but I have to go right now."

She got up, wiped a bit of anger-drool from her lips, and straightened her scrubs. Midge rushed to the hallway, turned back for one second to blow her daughter a kiss, and disappeared.

Nick blew out a giant sigh of relief when the door closed.

Holly turned to him. "Dad?"

"Sorry, baby. Your mom . . . she is a force of nature."

They both sat for a few moments in stunned silence. And then they just had to laugh.

Holly picked her arm back up. She moved it around in the same movements the doctor had. "I can't believe it doesn't hurt anymore," she said.

"They pumped you up with some serious drugs," Nick offered.

"Oh yeah," Holly said, and lowered her arm back down. "Is Mom coming back?"

Nick shrugged. "Jesus, I don't know, but I wish I knew that pager trick when we were married."

He picked a coarse hair off his shirt and frowned, realizing where it had come from.

"What do you think the dog is doing in your apartment right now?" Holly asked.

Nick frowned, and his stomach lurched a bit.

Holly laughed at her father.

"We can't go back there," he said.

"I'm sure it's not that bad," Holly said. "But you should probably call animal control."

"On myself?"

"Sure," she said.

Then the door to the room opened again. Nick braced himself, but it was only a nurse.

"We need the room. I'm terribly sorry," she said.

"What about my daughter?" Nick asked.

"What do you mean, sir?"

"My daughter?! She was bitten by a foaming-at-the-mouth rabid dog from the depths of hell??" Nick said.

"Were you not seen?" the nurse asked.

"No! I mean, maybe, for thirty seconds!"

The nurse was confounded. She flipped through her clipboard. "I don't understand," she finally said and looked to Nick for an explanation.

"The doctor came in, moved my daughter's hand in two circles, had a short yet terrible fight with my ex-wife, and ran out when you called in a code yellow on the intercom thing."

Holly nodded along.

"I'm terribly sorry," the nurse replied. She looked towards Holly's bandaged arm and gave a "looks fine" expression. "But we do need the room. If you can go back out to the waiting area, I'll let the doctor know where to find you."

---

They stood, dumbfounded. The same two chairs they'd sat in earlier were the only free chairs in the whole waiting room. A fresh cropping of tired families and crazies had cycled into the lobby.

Nick glanced around at the circus show. Then he leaned in towards his daughter's ear and whispered, "Do you feel okay?"

"Yeah, Dad."

"And you got that rabies shot, right?"

"Yeah, Dad." She glanced around the room.

A three-year-old ran past them swinging a play sword around at imaginary trolls.

"And you're not pregnant?" Nick asked.

"Of course not," she chuckled.

He nodded to the exit.

---

In his rush to get Holly to the hospital, Nick had forgotten to close his apartment door. Given the disaster the dog left, anyone walking past it likely assumed the place had been ransacked.

They inched their way through the mess just to make sure it was, indeed, empty before Nick could relax. The place was basically an insurance payout. Nick wondered if they could total an apartment the way they total a car.

Wallpaper hung in threads from the wall. Feathers from his pillows and comforter were everywhere. Cap'n Crunch was evenly spread across his entire kitchen floor. Nick had been in a frat in college and this was worse than every party they'd ever thrown all put together.

"Where do you think it went?" Holly asked. "The dog?"

"I honestly don't give one single shit. Thank god I left the door open."

"Do you think your neighbors . . ." Holly started.

"I-- I'm sure they're fine," he interrupted.

Holly grabbed a trash bag from the closet and with one good arm started cleaning up some of the debris.

"Holly, it's okay," Nick said. "It's four o-clock in the morning."

"I don't know about you," she said, "but I need to do something for a little while to calm myself down."

"Of course."

Nick watched Holly sift through his belongings on the floor. Unsure how to take the fact that she considered most of it worth trashing without asking him first.

"I like your apartment, Dad."

"What?" Nick asked, taken aback.

"Seriously," Holly said. "I think it's cozy."

She turned and started sorting through a pile of comic books that had been torn off a bookshelf.

Holly continued, "Mom's house is so big and empty. You're gone, and Mom is barely there. I never know what to do with myself. I have, like, two living rooms and all these spare rooms with nobody in them. Here is nice: couch, kitchen, bedroom. Simple."

Nick made a half-smile. He missed the simple, honest disarmament only your offspring could speak into you. "Sure, honey."

"I love you, Dad," Holly said. "It wasn't worth getting my arm almost torn off, but I'm glad I got to spend Christmas Eve with you this year."

The soft glow of the morning sun shone through miles of heavy cloud cover, several trees outside of Nick's apartment, and the broken venetian blinds on his window stirred Nick awake.

He opened his eyes just enough to see the mess of his apartment. They'd filled two bags of trash before passing out and still hadn't made a dent in the mess.

In his arms, wrapped in his blanket on his couch, was Nick's daughter. Exhaustion held him at enough of an emotional distance to keep him from weeping in the nostalgia, but Nick let himself imagine a tree filled with multicolored string lights and school-made ornaments sitting across from them.

The image made him smile, and he held Holly just a little bit tighter. He didn't know what the future held for their relationship, but he had right now, and that was everything. He smiled and closed his eyes.

And he almost didn't hear the sounds of the rabid dog and screaming elderly woman coming from the parking lot outside.

Ex Clans

In the last hours of Christmas Eve, all through the Brown home, everything was nice.

Quiet and still, except a few mice.

Kris Kringle soft-stepped, tip-toed across the roof. His concern wasn't children, but waking the woman who'd be home.

The one who left him. The only one he ever loved. The house he'd avoided for nine years. But tonight—maybe it was the pre-shift bourbon, but tonight was different.

He would be civilized. He'd waited until late to come. Everyone would surely be asleep. He would just drop a gift. Classy, not overly expensive, but a nice gift for her son.

Let her know he'd finally moved on and everything was okay.

A gift that said, "Sorry I was mad and started that fire in your old house. Sorry for gaining so much weight when I got this new job. Sorry for putting work before you. And sorry for trying to poison your peppermint tea the last time I saw you."

That last one he didn't really need to say, because she didn't know about it, but all the same.

Santa slid down the chimney, crawled out from a fireplace adorned with knitted, name-brand stockings, and looked around the living room.

Nice tree.

It was a *really* nice tree. Her husband must be loaded.

Fresh cut. Douglas Fir. Soft to the touch. LED string lights, all white. Beautiful, homemade porcelain ornaments. Carefully placed, high-quality, real-metal tinsel. And that gorgeous vintage star up top. That was all her.

How much better it must be with this new guy. This "husband" of only, what, six years? Someone who has money. Someone who gave her the opportunity to practice her art.

The place was covered floor to ceiling in crafts.

How lucky she must be. All the things he never could have provided for her. Wealth, taste, time, happiness, and a child, of course. Maybe it wasn't the only reason they broke up, but the infertility sure did its part.

Enough reminiscing. He was here to be suave and be gone.

James Bond in red felt.

Santa dug into his sack and pulled out a candy-cane red and white wrapped gift with a beautiful white satin bow on top. Inside, a leather-bound early edition of *A Christmas Carol* for the boy. It was a good choice. A book that suggested he was smart for almost ten. A Christmas book, but not one about Santa. It was rare *and* expensive.

He set the present under the tree and stepped back, bumping into the coffee table. There was an empty glass of milk and a plate with several cookie crumbs on it.

It sunk in that she'd had to fake Santa's visits for almost an entire decade now.

He sighed and took a big swig from his flask.

The mid-shift drink was almost better than the pre-shift one. Why hadn't he considered Bourbon Eve before? This was great!

The malty courage pushed him to explore a little more of the house.

Pictures lined the far wall leading to a staircase. It was a good collage of the family through the years. Too hard to look at any photos with the kid in them, but he did study a few photos of just his ex and the new guy.

Honeymoon in Hawaii. Happy, content. A more recent photo of a ski trip: she still looked great, still content. But was that it? Was she only *content* with this guy? Santa remembered her smile differently than it looked here. It had been brighter, fuller.

He was getting ahead of himself. You couldn't tell all that from a photo on a wall. Life is so complex. It's impossible to think the fraction of a second in which one photo is captured can reflect some great inner peace or inner turmoil. It could be a brief and unfortunate facial expression making you look depressed. Likewise, a rare smile could betray non-existent happiness.

Still. He did see something. In each frame.

There was something . . .

Without realizing it—deep in thought—Santa had climbed the stairs to the second floor. For his size, he was a quiet man. None of the stairs so much as creaked under him.

A small voice in his head asked, *why not just sneak a look?*

The hallway was full of closed doors.

*I'll have to check all of them to see which is the master suite,* he thought. *Just to get the quickest of glances at her. Then I will know for sure. By the way she is sleeping. If she is truly happy or not.*

Closet.

Laundry room.

Bathroom.

The next door was clearly the young boy's. A large video game poster hung on the outside of it. Santa decided to peek anyway. He was in too deep now to be timid.

The kid's room was awesome. The walls covered in film and game art. He was reminded of his own adolescence, posters of Led Zeppelin and *The Legend of Zelda*. Santa thought he could get along with this kid.

He closed the kid's door and walked up the hall to the next one.

The master suite.

There she was, the smaller of the two lumps in the bed. Meredith, his first and only love. He remembered how he'd wake up in the middle of the night back when they were together just to watch her sleep. She'd be curled up on her side, facing him. Mouth closed. A small, slight smile on her face. Quietly, beautifully resting.

*This* woman was on her back. Her mouth was wide open and snoring. He couldn't tell at first, because the guy was snoring too, but yeah, she was sawing some serious logs. Unconsciously, Santa side-stepped a laundry basket and ventured deep into the room. He was only a couple feet from her, studying her face.

Yeah, there were wrinkles where there used to be none. And her hair was frayed and thinner than he remembered, but god damn she was beautiful. He saw past the wide open, drooling mouth, the big, fat mouth guard and her double chin. She could be rigged up in a CPAP machine and she'd still be beautiful. Hell, she could be encased in an iron lung and he'd fall for her all over again.

He was leaning over her now. Inches away from her face. He'd been smelling her. Lavender. Mint. Sautéed onions.

She grunted and coughed. He realized she could probably smell him too, and the liquor on his breath. The thought brought him back to reality.

*What am I doing? I need to get out of here*, he decided.

He hurried toward the bedroom door before he could do something stupid, but in his rush he tripped over the basket of laundry sitting in the middle of the floor and fell on his ass.

Both sleeping adults bolted upright.

It could have been the shock of a stranger in the house, or the absurdity that he was in full-on Claus getup, but the two adults in the bed froze in silent terror.

"Fuuuuck . . ." Santa half-grunted, half-belched.

He tried and failed to get up.

Tube socks stuck to his felt jacket—he picked a pair of panties off of his shoulder and tossed them toward the basket.

"I'm so sorry, I was trying to find . . ." Santa began.

The husband kneeled on the bed and climbed in front of Meredith, between his wife and the rotund intruder.

"Hey! Hey! You!" the husband was repeating. "You! Stop! Out!"

Santa collapsed into a fetal position on the floor.

He was either displaying non-aggression, or his zero-budget

North Pole defense training was kicking in.

"Out, out, get out!" the husband continued.

It was loud, and annoying, but Santa was glad to see the guy obviously didn't own a gun or a baseball bat or nunchucks or something. He lifted his face up to look at the two adults in bed.

Meredith asked, "Oh my god. Kris? Is that you?"

Santa let out a sigh and rolled over onto his back.

" . . . yeah," he moaned.

"Who . . . what?" the husband asked.

"Frank, this is my ex-fiancé, Kristopher," she roared.

From the floor, Santa gave a wave.

"What. In the hell. Are you doing here?" Meredith continued.

"You know him?" Frank asked. Confusion. Anger. Sleep deprivation.

"Hey, Meredith." Santa burped. "Nice to meet you, Frank."

"Are you drunk?" Meredith asked from the bed.

"Yup," Santa answered. Still on his back.

Somehow more laundry had attached itself to his clothes. Long Johns. Tube socks. Frilly Christmas red and white lingerie.

"You can't be here," she said.

Santa rolled onto his side and grunted. "I know, I know."

"He . . . can't just break . . . can't just waltz in here . . ." Frank started.

"Quiet," Meredith begged her husband. "Please, for the love of god do not wake up the boy. Can you imagine?"

And just then the door creaked open. A boy stood in the dark of the hallway.

"Mommy?" he asked.

"Go back to bed, honey," Meredith said.

The boy didn't move. They all could hear him start to whimper.

"Hey, kid," Santa said. "How's it hangin'?"

The boy jumped. He hadn't seen Santa lying on the floor, camouflaged in laundry.

"Don't speak to him!" Frank yelled. He ran to the boy and picked him up. He then, *finally*, squared off to the plump intruder. The boy was in one arm, the other arm held up toward a still-collapsed Santa.

Frank took one small step forward. Moonlight reached in through the window and illuminated both father and son. Frank, as pale white, if not more so, as Meredith, and the boy, not . . . not Frank's kid. Santa gasped.

"What. The. Fuck."

His mind raced back to his final weeks with Meredith. Fights. Making up. Late-night fast food. Their small mattress. Fertility appointments. The abrupt ending of it all.

Sure, they were going at it like bunnies: angry sex and makeup sex and Tuesday sex and just-cause sex, but the doctor had said there was absolutely no way . . .

He'd only survived the breakup because there were no loose ends, no untied strings, nothing tying them together.

The tree in the living room shone bright and merry, oblivious to the emotions of the people sitting near it. All four of them sat around a pot of coffee that replaced the milk and cookies on the coffee table. Santa drank in big gulps, wishing—begging—for the miracle of sobriety.

"You can't be Santa," Frank said.

"Sure I can," Santa replied. "Didn't you see my big red sack?"

"Stop it," Meredith said.

"Meredith said your name was Kris," Frank said.

"Kris Kringle, you know, from that holiday jingle?" Santa replied. Meredith huffed.

The boy sat upright on her lap on the couch. He didn't stop staring at Santa. Santa couldn't stop staring at him either. The boy's mouth was wide open in absolute disbelief. Santa could see him pinching his own arm every so often.

Frank paced the room. The gears seemed to be turning in his head as he moved. He kept glancing up at Santa only to shake his head and continue pacing.

Finally he blurted, "Because you're black."

"And?" Santa asked. Amused.

"Well," Frank motioned to a Christmas ornament, "Santa Claus is white. Everyone knows that."

"Frank . . ." Meredith scolded.

"What?" Frank said.

"I am company," Santa began, "to a long tradition of important black cultural icons. Me. Jesus. Maya Angelou. George Washington Carver. Oprah. Kanye. Your god-damned kid is . . ."

"Kristopher, please, stop!" Meredith begged.

She held the boy tighter.

"What's your name, son?" Santa asked him.

"Like you," the boy said. "I'm Chris."

Frank hung his head. Defeat.

"Damn." Santa sighed.

He looked down at his empty cup of coffee. An inscription at the bottom of the inside of the mug read, "Be your own Christmas miracle!"

Santa had come prepared to drop a gift. Maybe, possibly, to give Meredith some kind of romantic speech, if he were to run into her. He was not prepared to meet her husband. Or her kid.

And he was absofuckinlutely not prepared to meet his own kid.

"I think it's time for you to go," Meredith said.

"Sure thing," Santa replied, crushed.

He stood and grabbed his sack, heading for the fireplace.

But he stopped halfway, looked over the wrapped presents under the tree, and picked up the present with a big white bow that it seemed he'd laid down here ages ago.

He placed it on the coffee table, motioning to the kid. "I brought this for you, son . . . err, boy. Kid, I mean . . . Chris."

"Thank you," Chris said. He grabbed the gift and unwrapped it.

Santa turned to the fireplace, his slow, dramatic exit. He kept an ear turned for some kind of response from the boy. Something to make it all worth it. Something to get him through the next twelve-million or so houses he had left for the night. A reason not to pitch poor Rudolph and his sleigh straight into the nearest rock outcropping and say goodnight to all.

Maybe they could get to know one another. Not now. Not fast, but give them a few years. The book could be a gentle reminder that somewhere out there, there was a man waiting . . .

Wanting to be known by his son . . .

There was a long silence after the wrapping paper was removed. Santa braced himself.

"Socks . . ." Chris said.

"What?!" Santa turned. "Ah shit."

Chris held an eight-pack of white tube socks. Size 5 with the two red lines stitched around the cuff.

Santa couldn't believe it. He frantically dug through the other gifts under the tree.

"Kristopher," Meredith said. "Stop it. Please . . ."

It didn't make any sense. The wrapping paper was right. The size was correct. Why didn't he feel the weight difference? Who gifts socks anyway? And where was that goddamned book?

Presents and tinsel flew as he dug under the tree.

Meredith walked over and grabbed Santa's arm. Her eyes were cold, distant. "Please."

Santa paused, her touch got to him.

A single tear swelled up in his eye and rolled down the left side of his face. Sparkling reflections of the tree lights and tinsel in the dim room.

Santa looked back at the boy. The ten-year-old kid stood silent, gripping Frank's hand. And Santa finally saw it: the two of them worked together. All three of them worked together. Those photos on the far wall, they were full of unbridled, absolute joy. They were a family and they were happy. No one in this house was desperately awaiting some sad gift from a make-believe stranger.

Meredith was happier here than she could ever have been with him. This was her place, and these people were her family.

He was the past.

Santa nodded, winked at the kid, and started again for the chimney. But this time he walked with confidence. He remembered who he was and knew his purpose. Time to get back to work. Let's bring the miracle of Christmas to those who need it.

"Stop." Meredith said.

Santa did.

Had she sensed his grand epiphany?

Was she going to invite . . .

She pointed away from the chimney. "For the love of god, do not make us watch you go up that chimney. Use the front fucking door."

Oh what Fun

Snow-dusted pine trees contrasted the wet, dark asphalt of the road. A fresh dump of powder in the backcountry quieted nature. Few birds passed overhead. Surely there were animals somewhere out in the woods, but right now everything was still and quiet.

Perfect.

The car sped along at sixty miles an hour. That elusive peacefulness of the road only existed for those inside, unaware of the noise and disturbance the two-ton vehicle moving eighty-eight feet every second made for everything outside of it.

Sufjan Stevens quietly sang along with the two men in the car:

> *Myrrh is mine; its bitter perfume*
> *Breathes a life of gathering gloom;*
> > *Sorrowing, sighing,*
> > *Bleeding, dying,*
> *Sealed in the stone-cold tomb.*
> > *O Star--*

The music muted with an incoming phone call.

"It's your mom."

"Later, I like this song," Fred said and moved to dismiss the call.

"Just get it," Arnold replied and hit the answer button.

There was a brief silence and the landscape outside again caught Fred's attention. The perfect coating of snow was breathtaking. How it took the sharp edge off every detail of the landscape and made it smooth, gentle. An even blanket covering everything in sight from aspens and pines across the road to rocky mountain faces miles away.

"Freddy?" Fred's mom said, breaking the silence.

"Hi, Mom," Fred replied.

"How's the drive, honey?"

"It's fine."

"The snow?" she asked.

"Also fine, everything is plowed."

"Good to hear, sweetie," his mom said. "Just be careful when you get to our neighborhood. Dad said the driveway was slippery and he has that big truck with the four-wheel drive."

"Okay, Mom," Fred replied.

"Is Arnold there?" she asked.

"Hey, Mom!" Arnold spoke up. "How are you? I hope you have that mulled wine on the stove already!"

"Oh dear, you're right! I haven't, but I will put it straight on. I forgot that is your Christmas drink, Arnold," Mom said.

Fred gave Arnold a look. "It's okay, Mom. We brought drinks. I'm sure you're busy."

"No worries, honey. It's Christmas day and if my son-in-law wants something special, he can have it!" his mom said, indignant.

"See you soon," Fred said, reaching for the end call button.

"Honey," his mom interrupted, lowering her voice, "your father is in one of his moods today. He's been in his shop all morning."

"Okay," Fred said, and hung up.

Arnold looked at him, astonished. "You are being rude."

"She's fine," Fred said and turned the music back up.

He let his mind escape back outside the car. The scenery he grew up with. The road they were on—a few thousand feet higher in elevation than Denver—surrounded by mountains thousands of feet higher still. Miles beyond the closest town.

Fred glanced around looking for elk. Still, calm, collected. There was no fear in those animals. No emotional baggage from their past. No stress or worry about anything that could be in their future. No social construct.

Just ten thousand years of evolution. A group of dutiful females, and one stud strong enough to carry the weight of the entire herd on his back.

"Sorry about your dad," Arnold finally said.

"He's fine," Fred said. "He can stay in the shop all day if he wants."

"Have you talked to him at all since last year? You spoke to him on your birthday?"

"Yeah." Fred swerved and didn't quite avoid a small pot-hole in the road. "He sort of congratulated me on getting to thirty-five. Then he said he wished he knew me better, and was about to get into some speech about manhood and I think he realized who he was talking to and kind of trailed off."

"And? Anything else?" Arnold asked.

"And I haven't heard from him since. Aside from the constant goddamn email forwards. Those will ever end."

"Sorry."

Their car went around an outcropping of rocks on the right side. Once past it, they could see more of the road and one long mountain face. Up the side of it ran a narrow, winding road. The road looked like it had been painted in by an artist. The trees lined it so perfectly, and it led to a huge building.

Both men looked up.

"Think we'll go back there before our tenth anniversary?" Arnold motioned to the restaurant disguised as a log mansion. The outside was old, original, a statement of Colorado heritage. The inside had recently been renovated and featured in every design and architecture magazine Fred knew of.

The pullout leading to it had a beautiful arched gate freshly painted, decorated with Christmas lights and a sign that read, "Oakmoore Lodge. Open Christmas Eve and Christmas Day."

"Hmm . . . it's probably bad luck to go back before our tenth," Fred responded.

"Are you serious?"

"No, I'm kidding," Fred said. "It's just such a long drive up here."

"And it's a special place for us . . ."

Fred didn't answer.

The road took another wide turn around the landscape, and the restaurant disappeared.

"Hello?"

"What?" Fred asked.

"Sometimes you disappear. Like your dad."

"No, I didn't. I don't," Fred shook his head.

"I'm trying to say that I'd like to go back up there sometime this year, maybe even before spring?" Arnold confessed.

"I know. OK?" Fred said.

"I didn't mean to . . ."

"You didn't. I just . . . If my mom knew we were all the way up here, she'd be sad we didn't visit her too," Fred replied. "Then I'd spend the whole meal feeling bad about it."

"We could always do both," Arnold argued.

Fred didn't answer again.

The road angled steep up towards the next valley. Fred's car started to make a whining sound.

Fred's tachometer made its way towards the red line, at only forty miles per hour.

"Your car, hon," Arnold said.

"I know."

"When was the last time you took it in?" Arnold asked. "All the way back in October?"

"No," Fred said before he could catch himself, "I never took it in."

"What?!" Arnold replied.

"It stopped making that clanking sound, so I thought we could just save our money."

"That's not how you save money with a car, Fred," Arnold said.

A beat-up old truck passed them in the left lane.

Fred caught the man's confused stare through the window as he passed them.

"That old man probably hasn't passed anyone uphill since he bought that truck in the sixties," Arnold said, then leaned forward and looked at Fred in the eyes. "Schedule an appointment for next week. I can't let you drive another car into the ground."

"Okay, Dad," Fred said and instantly regretted his word choice.

The hill steepened and the indicator dipped into the red line.

Fred knew Arnold was staring at the tachometer with his peripheral vision. He could see his husband calculating it against the incline of the hill, and all of it was pissing Fred off.

"You okay?" Arnold finally asked. "You seem edgy."

Fred shook his head.

Arnold reached into the backseat of the car, where they kept some granola bars.

"I'm not hungry," Fred stopped him.

"Okay, okay."

"My dad . . ." Fred began. "Maybe I should have just called in sick."

"Are you serious? You haven't seen either of them in a year."

Fred nodded. "It would be easier if I had siblings. If I could share him. Instead of getting the full brunt of it whenever I'm there."

"I'll be there too," Arnold offered.

"Yeah," Fred said, "but you know it's not like you help."

"What?"

"Well, it's just, I can change the conversation with him. You get all defensive. It's easier to just let him be," Fred continued.

The car crested the hill, and the whining quieted down.

Arnold looked out the window. "Your father hasn't said a nice word to you since I met you. He's probably *never* said a nice word to your mom. I love you both so much. It's impossible for me to just stand by silently while he says the things he does."

Fred nodded. "I know, but I just want to get this over with as fast and painlessly as I can. I would appreciate it if you let me talk and didn't engage."

Arnold gasped.

Fred continued, "My dad is my dad. I know he will never change—but you—you should know better. Don't spend the whole meal trying to egg him on."

"I need you on my side, Fred. Your mom needs you on her side. The fact that you choose to punish us for things your dad says . . ." Arnold trailed off.

"What am I supposed to do?" Fred asked.

"Well, you could start by accepting the fact that your dad hates that you're gay."

"Woah," Fred said.

"I'm serious," Arnold continued. "I never had parents to come out to, so I don't know how hard it has been for you, especially given your dad. I am so proud of you for doing it, but simply saying 'I'm gay' isn't some kind of magic fix to your family problems."

The sun peeked out from behind a thick curtain of clouds. The soft landscape around them sharpened. Hard shadows raked off the trees. It highlighted the jagged edges of the mountains surrounding them.

Arnold continued, "Coming out isn't supposed to be the last conversation, Fred. It's the first one."

Fred drove silently for several minutes.

They entered into a big valley. Snow banks stood ten feet high in some areas against the drift fences. The wind kicked up small flurries around them, magical in how unencumbered the snow became, spinning weightless for seconds, then drifting slowly to the earth, backlit against the sun. The moon was out, setting in the west ahead of their drive.

Below the moon, Fred saw a herd of elk. Miles away, he could see the stud standing erect. Guarding twenty or so females.

The animal's posture got under Fred's skin.

"My dad doesn't hate gay people," he finally said.

"Of course not," Arnold replied.

"No, seriously," Fred said. "he isn't a homophobe."

"I know."

"You don't know," Fred begged.

Arnold shouldn't have continued. "Fred, I really know."

Fred's eyes narrowed, confused.

"I mean . . ."

"You mean what?" Fred asked.

A Winnebago screamed by in the passing lane. The driver honked, and the rear tires dipped into a puddle of slush as it passed. It tossed a gallon of brown mud onto Fred's windshield.

He swerved—correcting—and hit the wipers, but there was no fluid. The blades smeared mud into a thin layer of brown on the windshield, making it impossible to see.

The world outside disappeared.

Arnold yelled and grabbed the "oh shit" handle above his own seat.

"It's OK!" Fred yelled.

"Pull over!" Arnold demanded.

Fred did, and they both exited the car. Arnold stepped straight into three feet of snow. He cursed.

"Do you know how dangerous it is to drive in the winter without wiper fluid?" Arnold asked.

"I didn't know I was out," Fred said. Then he went to clear the windshield with the arm of his sweater.

"Stop," Arnold said. "Let me do it."

Arnold bent and grabbed a flat chunk of clean snow from the shoulder of the road. He drug it across the windshield, washing away the brown sludge.

Another car sped past and let out a honk as it did so. Fred wasn't sure if the honk was to say "hang in there" or "fuck you!"

He slipped his cold hands into his pockets, sure that Arnold's strong hands must be absolutely freezing in the snow if his own were so cold yet dry.

"Arnold?" Fred asked. Quiet.

"You can wait in the car. I'm almost done."

"Why did you say that you're so certain about my dad?"

Arnold didn't answer. He just kept wiping the windshield.

"The way you said it," Fred said.

"Fuck." Arnold cursed under his breath and moved his hands to his face, blowing on them to warm them up. Fred walked over and took Arnold's hands into his own.

"Last Christmas your dad kissed me," Arnold blurted just as their hands met.

Fred let go.

"Yeah," Arnold said.

Fred looked at his husband. Arnold was not joking. Fred searched his serious eyes. His face. His lips.

All he could think to do was walk back into the car.

He looked at Arnold, who'd gone back to wiping the mud from the windshield. Careful and practical Arnold.

Fred wasn't furious as much as he was confused, angry, sad, and unsure. All feelings he—and Arnold—were too familiar with.

The thought brought a single tear to Fred's face, but he wiped it off immediately. He was still trying to act mad, confused as he was.

Arnold got back into the passenger seat.

They sat for a few silent moments, then Fred finally turned to Arnold. "How could you?"

"I didn't."

"But you must have put yourself in the situation. You had to have let him. You never told me! For a whole year?!"

"I know, and for the time it took . . . I'm so sorry," Arnold offered.

The road was quiet. Inside and outside of the car.

"How did he? I mean we were at the table for three awkward hours then we left to go home," Fred said.

"The kitchen. I'd gone in for more wine and your dad came in right behind me."

"But still," Fred said, accusing. "You just stood there . . . and took it?"

"I didn't! I pushed him away. It was all so out of left field. Never in a thousand years would I have thought . . ." Arnold stopped.

Fred turned the key, trying to turn the engine over.

The engine groaned and whined. It didn't start.

It only left them with a constant dinging reminder that the key was in the ignition.

"I just can't believe--" Fred said. "I wish you wouldn't have—"

"I didn't!" Arnold cried. "Your dad *me too*'d the shit out of me. He ambushed me!"

"Why would he even . . ." Fred tried, but he didn't have the words to finish his thought.

Arnold exhaled. "I don't know. Maybe he was confused? Maybe it was a brain misfire? Maybe it was some weird way for him to try and understand you?"

The pause between their thoughts hung heavy in the air. A gust of wind blew a cloud of snow over the road ahead.

A rancher in a giant red F-350 slowed to a stop next to their car. Arnold motioned to the window, and Fred rolled it down.

"You fellas okay?" the woman called from several feet above.

"We're fine, ma'am. Just had to wash off the window. Thank you," Fred said and went to roll his window back up.

"You Fred's son? Junior?" she asked.

Fred sighed under his breath.

"Yes, ma'am," he replied.

"Good to see you, it's been ages." She smiled, then she ducked her head a bit to see further into their car. "So this must be you, be your . . ." and she stopped herself, looking for the right word.

The two men joined her in the awkward silence. Unsure.

All they had was the obnoxious dinging of the key in the ignition and the loud rumble of the woman's diesel engine. The smell of exhaust floated into their car with help from the breeze outside. Memories of growing up here flooded back into Fred's mind. He wanted to be back in Denver. Back to where he was normal and not . . . whatever he was here.

Finally, Arnold interrupted the silence. "Nice to meet you. I'm Arnold, Fred's husband."

The woman didn't blink, didn't break eye contact. She took a short breath in through her teeth, nodded, and said, "Okay then."

Fred saw Arnold look to him for any kind of response.

"Say hi to your momma and poppa for me," the woman finished.

She waved. Drove off. And a dark cloud of diesel smoke from her tailpipe swept into their car before Fred was able to roll his window all the way up.

They coughed. Arnold opened his door in an effort to fan the smoke out of their car.

When it finally dissipated, Fed frowned. Almost a quarter of the way through the 21st century, and it seemed like some things were never going to change.

Fred looked from the corner of his eye toward Arnold. Neither spoke or moved. They both felt shame. Both angry with themselves for feeling it.

The road had now been quiet for several minutes. The elk Fred had seen earlier were making their way across the asphalt a hundred feet behind his car.

Fred watched in the rearview mirror as the bull led each member of his herd across the road.

Stoic, he guarded each individual as they crossed over.

The bull looked up and locked eyes with Fred. He was gorgeous. Massive. A thick, strong neck carrying a giant rack of antlers. Fred didn't know enough to count the points, but it had to be a prized bull. The bull kept eye contact with Fred until every last cow and calf made it to the other side. He was intimidating, like Fred's father, but behind *his* surly display was virtue.

Fred caught himself personifying the animal, but still, he savored in the moment.

The bull finally broke eye contact, crossed to the other side with his herd, and disappeared into the thick aspen.

"I'm sorry about my dad," Fred offered, starting the car.

It turned over immediately.

"I'm sorry too," Arnold replied.

And even though it wasn't much, it was something. And it was enough to get Fred out of his head for a moment. He swung the steering wheel hard to the left and turned away from the shoulder to head back towards Denver.

*Fuck my dad for once*, he thought, and he started the music back up.

> *Glorious now behold Him arise,*
> *King, and God, and Sacrifice;*
> *Heav'n sings Hallelujah:*
> *Hallelujah the earth replies.*
>     *O Star-*

Arnold looked at his husband after some time had passed.

The song had ended and they'd driven in silence for several miles. "You want to talk?"

"Yeah," Fred said.

And he made the turn onto a long, winding road leading to an old restaurant at the top of a mountain.

Gold, Frankincense and Sayda

Slaughtered presents. Maimed cardboard boxes. Tangled shreds of ribbons littered the floor in a ceremonious semi-circle. Three children sat, their presents all neatly sorted into individual piles. Two piles superior in both size and economic value. The third, out of place.

Sayda knew Christmas was about family, love, giving, and Jesus. She really did. But she was in seventh grade. So she also knew that it was about presents. And she knew that she'd been shafted.

Yet again.

George, her younger brother by three years, sat dwarfed by his pile of LEGOs. The sheer volume of his Christmas haul could justify building an addition to the house, just to store them. He was spoiled, but George was a good kid, and he was nice to Sayda. She felt a sisterly protection over him. She felt a sisterly love for him. And she had an immense jealousy of him.

Amy, Sayda's older sister by six months, sat cross-legged among her own presents. The majority of which were standard thirteen-year-old girl gifts. Makeup. Clothes. Fun socks. Gift cards. But in her lap sat her prized possession. The kind of gift you remember for the rest of your childhood, and likely for the rest of your life: a week-old pure-white bunny rabbit with deep red eyes and fur so soft, you could barely feel it on your skin.

Amy had campaigned for the bunny for the better part of a month leading up to Christmas. Even though George wasn't into pets without scales and Sayda was allergic, their parents still labeled the rabbit as a "family gift" and therefore didn't skimp on the rest of Amy's presents.

Amy was spoiled, but she had an air about her. It seemed like she deserved to be spoiled. Like the world actually revolved around her. Her teachers gave her special treatment. Her friends couldn't imagine a world where she wasn't the leader. Sayda gave her the eldest-sibling respect, but there was something else. Even if Amy were younger than Sayda . . . Amy would still be the center. Given this, Sayda appreciated that her sister occasionally put up with her. Occasionally let Sayda into her room. Occasionally sat near Sayda in the cafeteria.

Sayda had kept a running-total dollar value of her siblings' gifts as they opened them earlier that morning. She carefully recalculated each gift now, perusing the room. The exercise wasn't making her feel very good inside, but she needed something to fill the time. Socially, this was the "play with your gifts" part of the day. But Sayda had a problem, she couldn't actually play with any of her presents. Sure, this is an issue you come into at some point in your life, but hopefully many years after you turn thirteen.

She thought the wallet with a woven image of Frida on it was beautiful, but it gave her pause. Did her parents think Frida Kahlo was Guatemalan? Did they think Sayda was Mexican?

That morning, as Amy cried tears of joy upon seeing her bunny for the first time and George unwrapped LEGO after LEGO, Sayda opened a box containing a printout of her upcoming soccer tournament in Phoenix. Her parents explained that the family would take their spring break trip to Phoenix this year so Sayda could play with her team.

Yes, Sayda would have been devastated to miss the tournament, but she assumed this was a "non-special" activity. The family went to Palm Springs a couple months ago for Amy's basketball camp, and earlier that summer Amy and her mom had gone to Puerto Vallarta for a beach volleyball camp. Neither of those trips were classified as gifts.

Sayda decided not to count the value of her trip into her grand total, or, if anything, only to include her individual cost, not the entire family. With that taken into account, she figured her presents only held about a third to a quarter the value of her siblings' gifts.

Aside from the cash value, Sayda considered the emotional content of each gift between parent and child. Of the many "small" gifts Amy had opened, each told a story about something she'd asked for, something her mom "absolutely knew she would love" or something that represented a bonded attachment between the two of them. Each of George's gifts likewise reflected a sincere knowledge of his tastes and a deep love from his parents.

Sayda wasn't trying to be a sad Sally, but she felt her own gifts were based on half-assed thoughts two minutes in the making.

Things you'd find in the checkout lane of the store. Something convenient when you'd spent an hour looking for gifts for your oldest daughter and suddenly while you were paying for said gifts remembered you actually had not one, but two girls at home.

On the surface, Sayda knew that her parents loved her "just as much" as her siblings who were related to them by blood. But deep down she knew better. Even in progressive southern California, the looks she got when she was out with her family.

Biologically speaking, her parents owed her siblings more as honest-to-God *offspring* than they owed their mail-ordered daughter. Heck, the more Sayda read about adoption, the more she realized that she was likely not even a child they'd picked out, but rather one that was picked for them.

Sayda decided to think about something else. She looked around the room for a distraction.

"Hey, George! What *Star Wars* ship is that?" she asked.

"It's the Falcon," he said without looking up.

"Cool! What does it do?"

He didn't respond.

Sayda moved closer. "Can I help you build it?"

She grabbed a bag of small pieces not knowing it was open and accidentally spilled its contents onto the ground, mixing them with some other, carefully organized, pieces.

"No!" George cried and grabbed the bag from her. "Play with your own presents!" He huffed and dragged his arm across the ground, destroying his careful organization of all the other loose pieces in protest.

"Sorry," Sayda said.

"Go away!" he replied.

The two turned from each other. That pivot of their heads. For George, maybe, a small gesture.

Sayda looked over at her sister. Amy sat with the bunny, smiled, caressed and channeled her emotionally outbursting joy into a point of bright light shining throughout the entire room. Sayda knew her sister was far easier to get along with when she was getting her way. Maybe this would be a good time to connect with her.

"He's beautiful," Sayda said as she scooted next to her sister.

"She," Amy corrected.

"What?"

"She's a she. I know Dad said 'he' before, but I checked," Amy said.

Sayda could hardly see the bunny, Amy had it tucked so deep into her lap.

"Can I pet her?" Sayda asked.

Amy smiled. "No. She's sleeping."

"Okay." Sayda said.

She was about to scoot away, another failed attempt at Christmas-day camaraderie, but just then her nose tickled. Although she got ahold of her breath for a brief moment, reflexes got the better of her and she sneezed.

Loud.

The bunny jumped out of Amy's arms and landed in the middle of the room. Ears perked, and bloodshot eyes stared at Sayda in horror. Amy ran to her bunny and scooped it back up.

"Hey!" she said scornfully. "I said she was sleeping!"

"I'm sorry," Sayda said.

"You are so loud, Sayda! What's wrong with you?" Amy asked.

Sayda tried to apologize again. Her obnoxiously loud bodily functions were a sore subject to her parents and siblings alike.

"Ew!" George piped in. "Some of her snot flew all the way over here. Onto my pants!"

"Sayda, you're so gross!" Amy yelled. "You know you're allergic to pets, why would you even come over here?"

"Sayda's gross! Sayda's gross!" George was chanting.

Amy stood up and left the room with her bunny.

Sayda instinctively looked towards where her mother was, in the kitchen. But she stopped short from asking for help.

"Get along, children," or, maybe, "calm down," would be her mom's automatic response.

She looked busy.

Sayda dug through her stocking, then she picked up and unwrapped a chocolate orange. She ate one piece at a time and watched her brother reorganize his mountain of plastic bricks. The orange was gone before she realized, and she moved on to a pair of leggings. They were sparkly, blue, and decorated with soccer balls. She had to admit they were pretty cool, and they *were* soccer-themed. Maybe she'd give her parents one win for the season. She tore the tag off and stood up with them. Only then did she realize that they were at least two sizes too big.

Sayda frowned and put them back into the bag, wondering if they could be returned. It would be nice to get a ride to the store and find a similar pair that fit.

The sound of someone clearing their throat from the next room. Father.

He sat on his leather chair reading his new book. Sayda liked that big chair. Worn-down soft, soft leather, and a giant seat. The chair looked like it belonged in a British explorer's club. It wouldn't last forever, but Sayda could fit herself on the seat of the chair with her dad. It was her favorite place to sit in the whole house.

Her dad turned a page of the book and stroked the short stubble on his face. Sayda smiled, just being within eyesight of the wise, strong, lanky man calmed her.

She quietly walked up, placed a hand on her father's bony knee and asked, "Dad?"

He moved over to the side of the chair, opening up a spot for her.

She sat for a few minutes, halfway staring at the words on the pages of his book. Something about politics. Sayda couldn't remember if her dad was a Democrat or Republican, and the arcane language on the page wasn't giving her any clues.

After she squirmed for a minute, her dad put his book down and looked her in the eyes.

"Merry Christmas, Sayda," he said.

"Thanks, Dad," she replied. Without warning, two silent crocodile-sized tears rolled down her cheeks.

He took his left hand from the book and wiped both of her cheeks with the soft pad of his thumb. But the feeling of his strong, careful hands only made more tears come. Sayda had to clear her throat to make the embarrassing things stop.

"Sorry, Daddy," she said.

"What for?"

"I don't know," she said, meaning it.

Embarrassed, Sayda looked away from her dad and started to count all the red objects in the room. Something to distract herself out of her feelings. She didn't want to ruin the moment by sobbing.

"Did I ever tell you about the day we first saw you?"

"Yes, Dad. A thousand times," she said.

"Not the day we brought you home," he replied. "But the day we saw your picture for the first time."

Sayda didn't think so.

"Adoption is such a mess . . ." he began, stroking her hand. "We waited for you for several years. We waited so long that your mother forgot that she couldn't get pregnant and your sister was born.

Shortly before your sister's first birthday, the adoption agency called us and told us some of the best news of our lives. That they'd finally found someone for our family. You."

"Pancakes in five minutes!" Mom called from the kitchen.

Her dad continued, "It was the weekend. I had put Amy down for a nap, logged onto my email, and there you were. It was a picture of you at a park in Guatemala City. Your name was Sayda. You were beautiful. In a month I could come and meet you. One month! After how many years of waiting. Your mom and I cried. We cried and laughed and held each other for hours."

Her dad wiped another crocodile tear from Sayda's face.

"Your mom and I wanted a family so much. There were countless moments we didn't think we'd have any children at all. To be blessed in less than a year with not just one, but two beautiful daughters and then a few years later with a son? Sayda, I can't even begin to describe how much love we feel for you."

"Okay, come eat!" Mom called.

Sayda moved to get up, but her dad put one arm around her and tossed her hair with the hand on the other.

"I can't wait to see you play in your tournament. I know it's hard to wait for your gift, but planning your trip was by far the most fun your mom and I had with all of the presents. We love you, Sayda."

"Dad! It's time to eat!" George burst into the room waving around a half-eaten pancake.

Sayda's dad stood and lifted her up onto his hip. He picked up George with his other arm, and, with a loud grunt, walked them both to the kitchen table.

"Sorry I messed up your spaceship, George," Sayda said.

George looked at her with the ignorant bliss only a mouthful of buttermilk pancake drenched in Christmas-morning syrup can bring forth.

"Oh, whatever," he said.

Their dad slid George off his hip and into his seat at the table. He set Sayda in the next chair over.

George stood on his seat to reach the mountain of pancakes in the middle of the table.

"George, down," Mom said.

George sifted through the stack one by one until he found the biggest pancake and showed it to Sayda.

"Booyah," George said. "I already ate the biggest pancake, but you can have this one."

"Thank-" Sayda started.

George held the pancake up to his lips and licked it from bottom to top. Then carefully placed it down on Sayda's plate.

"Nasty!" Amy laughed.

Sayda laughed too.

She grabbed the syrup and poured a healthy amount on top of the slobbered pancake.

"You're so gross, George," Sayda laughed and dug in.

Merry Fucking Christmas

J ust outside of downtown, nestled into a corner lot, was the Dormer residence. A five-bedroom colonial complete with French country–style double swing-away front doors and circular driveway.

On those front doors hung an organic pine wreath, sustainably farmed and meticulously crafted by the finest artisan northwest of Chicago. Boughs of holly adorned the home's windows and framed the walkway up to the home, strung from candy cane posts. A Martha Stewart–approved snowman sat in the corner of the lawn ready to welcome approaching guests.

10 a.m.

Jeannie, the homemaker, busied herself inside, hard at work preparing Christmas dinner for her extended family. The turkey was frozen solid. All three boxes of instant potatoes in the pantry had been empty since Thanksgiving. And only three of her stove burners worked. Jeannie's husband, Steve, sat in the TV room working on an authentic 1800s post office for his model train set. He was somewhere between hungover and still drunk.

*Bling!*

Jeannie's phone buzzed. A text from her sister. "I'm running late. Can you preheat the oven to 425 for me?"

Jeannie looked at her oven. It was on. It was also full to the brim with sweet potatoes, cornbread, roasted veggies, and pumpkin pie.

"Mom!" Henry, Jeannie's ten-year-old son, walked in. "I've been up since five! Can we open presents yet?" He had a BB gun casually slung over his shoulder.

"Is your sister home yet?" Jeannie asked.

"How am I supposed to know?" he said. "I thought she was still sleeping in her room."

Jeannie sighed. "She spent the night over at . . . Lori's?"

*Or Mark's? Is it still Mark?* she asked herself.

"Jesus, Mom," Henry said.

The microwave dinged, and Jeannie retrieved a mug of coffee.

She looked at his gun. "No weapons in the house. You know that."

"It's not a weapon unless it's used for harm," Henry rebutted.

"Outside." She pointed with her coffee mug and then took a sip.

Henry was out. She'd have to worry about the BB gun later.

Jeannie looked around her kitchen. What else? Apps, check. Soup, check. Turk—damn. She grabbed a spoon and tapped it on the frozen bird's breast. *Clink.*

She checked the oven again. Still full. She wondered if the roasting pan would cook on top of the range without starting a fire.

Then she glanced at the microwave. The defrost button looked like a get out of jail free card.

Something cracked outside. Jeannie walked to the kitchen window to see what it was.

Henry walked into view of the window. With, of course, the BB gun. "Be careful out there, Henry," Jeannie called.

He gave her a thumbs up.

"Hon!" Steve called from the TV room. "Where are all my silver metallic paints?"

"I don't know, dear," Jeannie called back.

"Well, I can't finish the post office without them," he whined.

Jeannie didn't care to continue with him. She moved a boiling pot of water off the burner, forgetting what was supposed to go inside of it.

Another crack from outside. Jeannie didn't turn this time. And she didn't hear the faint thud either. A squirrel bounced off the roof and dropped to the ground with a pellet-sized hole in its head.

"Hon! Did you hear me?" Steve called again.

"Steve. I'm busy," Jeannie said.

"My paints!" he bellowed.

"You are the only person who touches those paints, Steve. And you had them all last night." She tried not to let her voice crack.

"Well, I don't know where they are now! Seriously. I only get one day off for Christmas and I'm going to spend it looking all around for goddamn paints. What a waste." He grunted and raised the volume of the TV significantly.

12 p.m.

The front door swung open and Jeannie's sister, Suzan, walked in. She plopped three—almost frozen—casserole dishes onto the counter, sailed an empty venti-size coffee cup into the trash, and squatted next to the oven to see through the glass.

"Hey, girl," Suzan said. "How are you doing?"

"I've got problems, girl," Jeannie replied. "Turkey problems. Potato problems. Son. Daughter. And . . ."

"For the love of god . . . Personal foul!" Steve shouted at the TV.

Jeannie sighed. "I need you to figure out how to thaw and cook this turkey, immediately."

"Fair enough," Suzan said. "What else?"

Jeannie laughed. "Figure out which boyfriend my daughter stayed with last night. Take away my son's BB gun before he kills himself. And change your boyfriend's skin color from brown to white, just for this one meal, then you can change him back. Pretty please?"

"Jeannie," Suzan said.

"Sorry. I am stressed, girl," Jeannie said, and her phone started to ring. "Grandma--" she mouthed to Suzan.

Suzan slunk out of the kitchen.

Jeannie answered her cell on speakerphone anyway.

"Hello," Jeannie started, but there was nothing but garbled noise on the other end.

"Mrhhpmh, cough, yess . . . Oh my, narhhh."

Jeannie waited.

"Jeannie, are you? Argh this confounded contraption. I better not be on the face call…"

"Grandma. Hi, I'm here. How are you?" Jeannie said.

"Fine, fine. Look, don't let any of your food burn on the stove."

"Sorry?" Jeannie asked.

"While you're on the phone with me. Don't forget to keep an eye on the meal."

"Oh, I'm standing right here in the kitchen, Grandma."

"I'm sure," Grandma said. "Just, this year, check on those pota-toes from time to time, okay, hon?"

"Okay, Grandma."

"Should I be prepared for a surprise this evening, Jeannie?"

"No surprise," Jeannie said. "Just family and dinner."

"I'm an old woman, Jeannie. This heart can't take surprises."

Jeannie looked to her sister for help. But Suzan was just coming back in, dragging a cooler from the garage.

"Look, Grandma," Jeannie said. "We're all very excited to see you. Why don't we talk more when you get here?"

"Well, I'd never—" Grandma started.

"Hey there, Suz . . ." Steve said from the doorway. He held a large cup of ice, bourbon, and maybe an ounce or two of cola. His droopy eyes lingered.

"Hi, Steve," Suzan said back.

Jeannie was shooing Steve away with her hand like a dog while she spoke. "Grandma, I love you. We will see you really soon."

"Jeannie, is that Steve? Is Suzan there? I'd like to talk to her," Grandma continued. And it sounded like she *growled* a little.

"Is that your grandma? What does she want?" Steve asked.

"Shh," Suzan warned and snapped her fingers at him.

"I want to speak to Suzan," Grandma called from the speaker.

Suzan backed up into the corner, her eyes wide, like trapped prey.

"Bye, Grandma," Jeannie said and hung up the phone.

The two women let out a sigh of relief. Suzan lifted a kettle of hot water off the stove and poured it into the cooler she'd just brought in.

"I like those pants, Suz," Steve said.

Jeannie rolled her eyes, "Get out, Steve."

"Come on, Jeannie," Steve said. "Last time your sister was here you told me I didn't say anything nice to her. Here I am. Saying nice things."

"Enough, Steve," Jeannie pleaded.

They all heard the front door open.

"Gretchen?" Jeannie called.

"Hey, honey." Steve's posture changed as their daughter walked into the kitchen.

"Hi, Dad." Gretchen kissed her father.

Steve winked one last time at Suzan and left for the TV room.

"Good to see you around these parts," Jeannie said to her daughter, ignoring her husband.

"You too," Gretchen offered back, sarcastic.

"Hi, Gretchen," Suzan said and gave her niece a big bear hug. "You have a good night?"

"Yeah, sure," Gretchen said. "Just hung out with some friends."

"Sure you did," her mom said from the stove.

"Mom . . ."

Suzan went back to her cooler project, pouring another pot of boiling water into it. "You still seeing that boy?" she asked. "Peter?"

"No, Aunt Suzan. We broke up a couple weeks ago,"

Suzan grabbed the frozen turkey and dropped it into the boiling cooler. A bit of water splashed onto her shoes.

"That's right. Is it Mike? I'm sorry I can't quite keep up?" Suzan continued. She stole a glance at Jeannie.

"No, not him." Gretchen dug through the fridge. "Is there no more pizza in here?"

"I don't know, hon," her mom sighed. "When's the last time you ate?"

Another crack from outside. And the sound of another small body hitting the roof and tumbling down to the yard. The squirrel fell directly past the window, but no one inside saw.

"Henry!" Jeannie yelled.

The boy's head popped up in the window.

"Gretchen!" George smiled at his sister.

Gretchen went back to the fridge.

Jeannie called through the window, "No more BB gun. I'm taking it!" But Henry was already inside the kitchen with them.

"Presents!" he said.

"What is in that bag?" Jeannie asked, looking at a black trash bag the boy held in his hand.

"Presents-- err, nothing, Mom. Gretchen is home! That means we can finally open Christmas presents. Come on!" Henry said.

He casually tossed the bag into the freezer.

"What is in that bag young man!" his mom said again.

Gretchen reeled. "It smells gross!"

It did.

Henry slammed the freezer door shut, and pointed to the clock. "The day is almost half over. I've been up since before dawn waiting to open my gifts. You told me to wait until Gretchen came home. She's home. I want to open my presents!"

"Everyone but you is busy getting dinner ready for the family, Henry," Jeannie rebutted. "Get rid of that BB gun and take a shower. You're covered in snow and mud. We'll open presents later."

"Later. Later. Later." Henry stomped his feet.

"Out!" Jeannie cried.

Henry surrendered and walked out of the kitchen. "I know where they are anyway. I should just open mine alone since you all suck at life, and Christmas."

"No more BB gun!" Jeannie called upstairs, then to her sister, "That boy. I swear on my life."

"I guess I'll just eat some carrots and ranch dressing like an impoverished rabbit," Gretchen sighed and walked to the TV room.

"You haven't done presents yet?" Suzan asked.

Jeannie looked at her sister. "No, I haven't done presents yet, Suzan." Her face was red.

Steve called from the TV room, "Your daughter just turned on *TV's Sexiest Christmas Moments*."

Suzan stifled a laugh. Then, seeing her sister's face redden more, she went back to poking at the frozen turkey in the cooler. They still hadn't made any progress.

"Gretchen has been home a grand total of maybe ten hours this entire winter break," Jeannie started. "She won't tell me who she's with or when I may see her again. I felt like I had to beg her to be home at all today. My husband is only off for a few days and he plans on spending the entire time asleep or drunk. My son is turning into African-Safari Teddy Roosevelt, and I don't know what to do with him. I am four hours into a dinner that isn't working, and every time someone here opens their mouth they criticize me. So no, we have not done presents today. I'm considering putting them all in the middle of the cul-de-sac, emptying a couple gallons of gasoline onto them, and burning a sacrifice to god or satan or Elf on a Shelf or whoever can make this last week of the year not as shitty as the previous fifty-one."

"Burn the gifts, or your family?" was all Suzan asked.

"Either."

Jeannie wiped a pity tear from her cheek and started to fill the already packed dishwasher.

"Don't be such a drama queen, girl. You'll be fine," Suzan said with a smile. "Bad year for Mom and Dad to be out of town, huh?"

Jeannie answered, "It's good practice. I just didn't think it would be this level of a shit-show hours before anyone even got here . . ."

Buzz.

The phone interrupted again.

"Grandma," Jeannie said.

"I got it," Suzan said and put it on speaker, "Hi, Grandma!"

"I'm in the car with Alice. I wanted to let you know that I forgot to bring her something to eat."

"Oh, hi," both Jeannie and Suzan said in unison.

Neither of them knew an Alice, but Grandma seeing dead friends in her car was nothing new.

Grandma shouldn't have been driving in the first place, she could barely see ten feet in front of her, but she liked to be independent and it wasn't like anyone was chomping at the bit to cart her around greater Illinois.

"I've been thinking about your secrets," Grandma said.

"Okay. We can talk later tonight about it," Suzan interrupted.

Her voice cracked a little.

Jeanine went to take the phone off-speaker, but she was too late.

"Suzan, you have greatly disappointed me. To publish a photo—kissing a man. Locking lips. Interracially! On the internet site, for anyone to see—"

Jeannie hung up.

It was Suzan's turn to wipe a pity tear from her face.

"Don't be such a drama queen," Jeannie said with a wink.

"Okay," Suzan took in a deep breath, "Where do we stand on the food? Give me a to-do list."

"Well," Jeannie started, looking around, "turkey is still priority number one. I own three empty boxes of mashed potatoes, so we don't need to worry about that."

"Gravy?" Suzan asked.

"I planned on making it from the turkey drippings, but it's not looking like that's an option now. Somewhere in the pantry I have a couple cans of instant gravy."

"Okay I will start," Suzan said. "Is that really a thing? Instant?"

"I don't know. Just look for some," Jeannie pleaded. "What do we need to do for the bird?"

"I'm pretending the cooler is helping it thaw," Suzan said. "But we probably need a different plan."

She looked over, and Gretchen was back in the kitchen. A small broccoli tree hung from her mouth in exasperation.

"Mom? Are you thawing the turkey in a plastic cooler?" Gretchen balked, eyes wide.

"Yes," Jeannie sighed.

"Do you know anything about BPA's? You are literally giving that turkey a cancer bath!" Gretchen said.

"Please don't give the turkey cancer, Jeannie!" Steve called, sarcastically, from the TV room.

"It's fine!" Jeannie yelled. "We're taking it out to try something else."

"It's probably too late already," Gretchen said.

Suzan sighed, pulled the turkey out of the cooler, and dropped it onto the counter with a frozen thud. Several ounces of salmonella splashed from the impact onto everything nearby and several more dripped over the side of the counter and onto the floor.

"What the hell is going on in here?" Steve mumbled as he walked in and over to the freezer. He brushed aside a black trash bag and grabbed a handful of ice cubes for his glass.

"How many of those are you up to?" Jeannie asked.

"Last one right here." Steve raised the glass in a mocking cheers. Then he pointed to the counter behind them, "Turkey . . ."

The frozen turkey was sliding down the uneven countertop like a hockey puck. Suzan grabbed it just before it slid off onto the floor.

"What are we going to do?" Suzan asked.

"I can order some pizza right now," Gretchen said and went for her phone.

"No," Jeannie snapped. "Steve, you go get that carving knife and an extension cord."

Suzan leaned over, studying the solid bird. She knocked on it with her knuckles and pulled her hand back. "That actually kind of hurt," she mused.

"I've got a better idea," Steve said. "Don't move."

He hurried to the garage.

The doorbell rang.

"Get the door, Gretchen," Jeannie said. "And Suzan, you need to get me four dishes out of that cabinet over there that can hold a quartered bird."

"Gross," Gretchen said.

"Yeah," Suzan added.

"There's no other way," Jeannie muttered and gave them all what she thought of as a very "Henry" glance.

"Hello?!" A loud voice came from the front door. "It's Uncle Jack. I'm just gonna let myself in!"

Uncle Jack carried in a half-empty plastic bottle of whiskey. He stomped his wet boots onto the floor mat and proceeded directly to the couch in the TV room. "I'm turning this trash to the game."

"Mom . . ." Gretchen protested.

"Jeannie!" Jack continued unseen. "You got any apps cooked up yet? I'm starving!"

"Jack!" Steve yelled on his way back in from the garage.

"Hey, bro!" Jack yelled back.

Steve slammed a dusty and muddy Sawzall down onto the counter and slid the battery into the tool like he was loading a gun.

"See here, Suzan. Just pull the trigger and hold on to it for dear life. This thing'll turn that frozen bird into the Donner Party!" Steve smiled.

"Gross," Gretchen said and walked back to the TV room.

The blade of the Sawzall was rusty and peppered with sawdust. Suzan grabbed the tool and got to work. Pieces of half-frozen flesh broke off the turkey and flew around the room.

Jeannie flicked a penny-sized chunk from her shirt. "Thanks, hon," she said to Steve.

Steve returned to the TV room. "Jack! You son of a bitch! How in the hell are ya?"

Jeannie watched the dismemberment of the turkey another ten seconds before she registered a growing sound from the stovetop as boiling water. *What would be boiling now?* she thought.

"The stuffing!" Jeannie said and took the lid off of a pot on the stove. Chunks of stuffing boiled out of the pot and onto the stove. Jeannie pulled out a colander in a panic and started to strain the soggy stuffing dumplings in the sink.

Seeing an opportunity, Henry tiptoed back into the kitchen and placed another object into his freezer trash bag. He carefully slunk back out unnoticed.

Suzan had the turkey in half and started to work on quartering it. She grabbed the torn plastic bag of gizzards that she'd just finished sawing through and tossed it into the trash.

"Jeannie!" Steve called from the other room. "Metallic paints! Don't forget!"

Jeannie ignored him and spread the soggy stuffing onto a cookie sheet. When she opened the oven, her sister scolded her. "Don't! I need all that space for the turkey! I'm almost done!"

Shards and chunks of turkey decorated Suzan's entire upper body and sprinkled her hair.

Suzan pried one of the pieces apart, set it into a glass bowl, and placed the bowl into the microwave. She punched in the instructions for a forty-five-minute thaw and clapped her hands together triumphantly like she'd just solved global warming.

"Alright!" she said.

"Suzan, you can't just--" Jeannie started.

"Can't what?" Suzan replied. "Can't *thaw* the turkey? This is perfect. It will work!"

Suzan took a second quarter of turkey and placed it back into the boiling cooler. She grabbed a third and tossed it into the oven. She held the final quarter for a moment, spinning around, looking for somewhere to put it.

Thud!

Suzan ditched it into the trash can. "Casualty of war," she said. "Three out of four isn't so bad."

Again, Jeannie wanted to protest, but couldn't think of a better solution. She went back to her stuffing.

2 p.m.

Henry stormed into the kitchen. "Mom!"

Jeannie was furiously chopping onions with her back turned. She didn't acknowledge the sound.

"Mom! Mom, look at me!"

More onions died in the fury of the exhausted and pissed off mother, cook, and homemaker.

"Jeannie, stop!" Henry said.

"What?" she said, and turned.

Henry walked straight up to his mother, looked her in the eyes, and put a hand on each of her shoulders. "It's time to open presents. Once the rest of the family gets here I won't have a chance. Not until tomorrow. The . . . day . . . after . . . Christmas. The 26th of December. You can't make me wait until tomorrow, that's child abuse!"

"Henry," she sighed, "I'm sorry, there's just no time."

"I know where they all are, just let me open one present on my own. I can wait 'til tomorrow for the others."

He dropped to his knees. "Please, Mom, please, it's all I ask! Please! Please!"

"Fine," Jeannie said and turned back to the onions, "Just one."

Henry bolted to the stairs.

"And don't you touch anything else up in the attic!" Jeannie called after him.

"The attic! Of course." Henry said from far up the stairs. The sound of the stowaway ladder crashed above them. It sounded like ten kids were upstairs instead of one.

Ding dong!

The doorbell rang. Jeannie looked at her sister. They both knew who it had to be.

Jeannie opened the front door and let out a sigh of relief. Still no Grandma. A few more family members (cousins, uncles, aunts, no one important) walked in with a quiet hello to Jeannie. She shuffled them all in from the cold and was pushing another man inside when he protested, "Jeannie! It's me, John, your neighbor?"

"Oh. Hi, John," she said.

"Look, Jeannie, I know it's Christmas, and you have family over, so I don't want to bug you," he said.

"Of course, thank you," Jeannie said and started to shut the door.

"Wait. Jeannie, I have to talk with you for a second," John said.

Jeannie tried to concentrate. "Yes, of course, sorry."

John motioned toward his house. "Our front window was broken this morning."

"Oh no, so sorry to hear it. Did anything get taken?"

"No. No it wasn't broken like that. I think someone threw a rock through it. Maybe," he said.

"Oh," Jeannie replied, then realized, "Oh!"

She lost a little color in the face.

"Can you maybe just talk to him about it and see if he knows anything?" John asked.

"Of course, John. I'm so sorry."

"Thank you, and Merry Christmas," John said and turned home.

Jeannie shut the door and turned to face the direction of her impossible child. She yelled all three of his Christian names.

He ran downstairs wearing an oversized leather jacket (a gift from Jeannie to Steve this Christmas) and a much-too-small Superman costume (Halloween 2012), and he held a five gallon bag of candy (Easter 2015).

"Henry . . ." she started.

"It's okay, Mom, these don't count as Christmas presents, they were just sitting around up there." He tore the tag off of the Superman costume, ripping some of the fabric with it.

"Child . . ." again she was interrupted.

"Sorry, Mom, I need to get back up there. I still haven't opened any of my presents."

"One present," Jeannie started. "No, actually, no presents. You didn't listen to me. That jacket is for your father. That candy has got to be a few years old. And, and, and . . . Did you throw a rock through the neighbor's window!?"

Henry looked at her, aghast. "No way! I don't throw rocks!"

She tried to process his face. He didn't look like he was lying. Then, over his shoulder, resting on the top of the stairs, she saw it, the BB gun. "Oh, Henry," she said.

He followed her gaze until he made the same realization.

"Oh shit," Henry said.

"Yeah," Jeanie started.

"Jeannie! Where are all the apps?" Steve yelled from the kitchen. "We're starving here! Your niece is hypoglycemic, remember? We need food, *literally*, for her health."

Jeannie glared at Henry, and he took it as an exit cue.

"Jeannie? Where you at?" Steve called again.

"Lord Almighty!" Jeannie mumbled on her way to the next fire. She walked into the kitchen, where three people were raiding the fridge and pantry. Suzan was unsuccessfully trying to fight them off.

"Hey!" Jeannie called, "Not now, wait for dinner, all of you!" She swung a spatula at the crowd, warding them off. The relatives dispersed out of the kitchen, and Jeannie looked around to see if they left her anything to cook with. That was when she noticed that the microwave was off.

Suzan threw a couple wet paper towels into the trash. "Fire," she said, "nothing to worry about. But I think your microwave is totally out of commission."

Jeannie saw the charred mark on the wall above the microwave.

"While you were at the door it sparked and there was smoke. I thought maybe I'd put the settings in wrong. So I reset it and tried it again, but then there was an actual fire. A big one."

"Jesus, Suzan," Jeannie said.

"I know," Suzan replied.

The fridge swung open again and Gretchen was back. She had three beers, one soda, and a stick of salami in her arms.

"Gretchen?" Jeannie said.

"They're not for me. Obviously, Mom."

"No more snacks for you," Jeannie said, grabbing the salami. "You need to wait for dinner. I'm not slaving away here so you can fill up on snacks before we sit down at the table."

Gretchen looked around the kitchen. Smoke tendrils spun from the microwave, the oven light was on and she could see the quarter of turkey oozing through the shelf grates inside. There was a plate of cold, mushy stuffing on the counter, and more food was inside the trash can than out.

"Right," Gretchen said, adding as she left. "Tell that to everyone in the TV room. They just ordered a ton of pizzas."

"You okay, girl?" Suzan asked.

"Yeah, sure," Jeannie replied.

The doorbell rang again. This time Suzan left to answer it.

She took in a deep breath and opened the front door. It was Grandma. And Alice . . . who, it turned out, wasn't an imaginary, long-dead friend, but a giant orange cat.

The cat jumped through the doorway and ran to somewhere deep in the house.

"I want to meet this exotic of yours," Grandma blurted.

"Grandma!" Gretchen called and ran in to hug her grandma. She had an open beer in her hand.

"Thanks for coming, Grandma," Suzan said, helping the ninety-four-year-old in, and closed the door.

A little more commotion exploded from the kitchen and Suzan took it as an excuse to exit the foyer. "Make yourself at home," she said, walking away.

"No, dear, no. I must come and supervise," Grandma said and followed with her coat and shoes still on.

As they crossed the hall, two gunshots rang out from upstairs.

"What is that god-awful racket?"

"Just Henry and his BB gun," Suzan said.

"That's no pellet gun," Grandma replied. "That sounds like a rifle from the Great War."

The kitchen was a frenzy and only one person was inside. Jeannie cursed with anguish as she removed the turkey from the boiling cooler water. She wiped it down with a hand towel, placed it onto the same cookie sheet as the stuffing, and crammed it at an aggressive angle into the last space in the oven.

"My god," Grandma started, but then she slipped on some uncooked risotto on the floor.

---

4 p.m.

Grandma sat on a chair in the corner of the kitchen. She was a fragile old woman who'd just fallen, but she was also an unwelcome, salty chef de cuisine crossed with a villain from a Cormac McCarthy novel. Jeannie and Suzan were furiously plating the dishes they'd been preparing for hours. Everything got butter, garlic, or cheese on top to hide bland, bad flavor and/or burn marks. Both women unconsciously had their backs turned to their grandma.

"You know I have a low tolerance for salt," Grandma said as Jeannie seasoned the Brussels sprouts, "and, Suzan, those potatoes are probably getting cold sitting over there by the open window."

"Okay, Grandma." Suzan sighed.

A loud cheer from the TV room.

"Oh, my back," Grandma groaned. "Who leaves dangerous food like that on the floor?"

Jeannie plated faster and faster. She could only hope that sitting at the dinner table with the whole family would somehow make it all worth it, but . . . well.

"It's a kitchen, not a grain silo. You do own a broom don't you?" Grandma said, rubbing her ankle.

The doorbell rang again and Suzan ran to it. Enrique was late, but at least he came. The one bright point in this shitty holiday was that he had to suffer right alongside her.

But when she opened the door it wasn't Enrique looking at her with longing in his eyes, it was the pizza delivery boy.

"Wow," he said.

"Sorry?" Suzan replied.

He was too young to be creepy, but he wasn't charming.

"Sorry, I just . . ." he started. "I mean the Christmas Day shift is a real self-harm-inducing seven hours, but my god, you are so beautiful it almost makes it all worth it."

Suzan blinked away a smile growing on her lips.

"So this all comes to $132," he said, handing over a stack of pizzas.

"What?" Suzan snorted.

"Four pies, convenience charge, and tax. $132."

"Convenience charge?" she asked.

"Sorry, ma'am, Christmas Day and all. It's like an extra tip." Then, seeing her expression, he said, "But it doesn't go to me. I still need- - er, would appreciate a tip."

"Jesus, Mary, baby Jesus, Joseph, ass, god loving . . ." Suzan mumbled and took a wad of cash out of her purse from the coat rack just inside the front door.

The delivery boy laughed. Suzan looked up to scold him, but seeing the smile on a face that otherwise would be having a shit day hit her in the funny bone.

She started to laugh too.

She wiped a tear from her eye and handed over the cash, "Merry Christmas," she smiled.

"Sure thing," he said, then looking around for eavesdroppers, he lowered his voice. "The pizza is, like, really bad. Especially today. No one back at the pie shop wants to be there on Christmas either. I'd let your guests have it to themselves if I was you. Especially the Hawaiian." He laughed again and left.

Suzan closed the door with her back and leaned against it for a moment. Four people ran in from the TV room, each grabbing a box. They ran out as fast as they'd come without so much as a thank you to her.

Another loud bang from upstairs. Jeannie cursed and sprinted up to the second floor. There was yet another bang and some loud words, then Jeannie returned with the BB gun in hand. She hid it on top of the armoire next to Suzan in the entryway.

"My baaack . . ." Grandma groaned from the kitchen loud enough for them both to hear.

Jeannie walked into the kitchen. "You better start making your way to the dining room, Grandma. Suzan is setting the plates now. I have a feeling it might take you a while to get all the way there."

"Jeannie Ann," Grandma said.

Jeannie didn't respond. She took an armful of dishes into the dining room. "Dinner!" she called.

Suzan set the table. She tried not to think about the mismatched bowls and stained napkins. She heard a strange noise from underneath one of the chairs.

It was Alice. Alice had a large slice of Hawaiian in her paws. She hissed at Suzan.

"You little bitch," Suzan mumbled under her breath.

She reached for the pizza and got ahold of a corner. The cat groaned a deep groan and then took a swipe at Suzan's hand. It missed, but the look on its face . . . Suzan had never seen such evil.

"This house is drafty," Grandma complained from the hallway.

"Gretchen, come help your great-grandmother into the dining room," Jeannie called.

Suzan hurried back to the kitchen and tossed a box of pizza into the freezer, failing, or not caring enough, to shut the freezer door all the way. She ran her hands under the faucet in the kitchen, feeling a need to wash the cat from them.

She and Jeannie danced around each other with casseroles for another ten minutes before they'd finally emptied the kitchen into the dining room.

When Jeannie brought the last dish to the dining room, almost everyone had found their seat. Most of them had slices of pizza on their plates, but it may have been for the best. Steve was still in the TV room, snoring. She decided to leave him be.

But her son . . .

"Henry," she called, "come downstairs and eat with your family."

Grandma was just about to the table. She'd take one tiny step, a deep breath, a sigh, and then another tiny step. This was tradition.

Why should any of them eat on time when Grandma had so many things to muse on and complain about on her way in.

"These aching feet. If only you had carpet in your house like a civilized—*sigh*—and all of you, when was the last time someone in this family wore a tie or a dress—*sigh*—where is this illegal man I was told to expect—*sigh*—aren't there less people here?" She paused at this and looked over the faces in the dining room. Counting.

"Did somebody die since last year?" she finally sat down.

"Steven, would you like to say grace for us . . ." she started and his snores from the other room interrupted. "Oh . . ."

"It's okay, Grandma. I will," Jeannie said, excusing her husband.

"No, dear. You wouldn't even know how," Grandma said. "I will invoke the blessing."

Suzan sighed.

"Dear Lord Almighty, one and only, precious, wonderful one. How many blessings can one humble servant of yours say thanks for in ten minutes," Grandma started. Her voice changed to an almost-mocking theatrical tone.

Jeannie wondered where people learned to pray like that.

The blessing went on. And on. The family members at the table individually prayed for a short ten-minute blessing.

Or, ideally, a medical emergency.

"And forgive any members of my family and extended family who may have fornicated or committed adulterous thoughts or actions . . ." Grandma was interrupted by the front door opening.

"*Feliz Navidad*, everyone!!" Suzan's man, Enrique, bellowed from the foyer.

"Oh Christ!" Grandma shrieked.

Enrique held his million-dollar smile. "I am so sorry to be late and to interrupt dinner with my arrival."

"You didn't interrupt dinner, you interrupted the blessing," Grandma said, stomping her foot.

"It's okay," Suzan said, and ran up to Enrique, giving him a hug.

"Come sit, you two," Jeannie said. She grabbed the carving knife and started for the best-looking quarter of turkey.

Grandma blew out a long, audible retort. It sounded like the iceberg that cut through the hull of the Titanic. "We have not finished the blessing!"

"Of course," Jeannie said, and sat.

Suzan and Enrique walked towards the table. The extended family watched the lovers approach. Oblivious to the attention and the hostility of the family, Enrique leaned over and kissed Suzan on the cheek.

"Oh my god!" Uncle Jack blurted.

The two stopped in their tracks. Embarrassed. Appalled.

Suzan opened her mouth to protest but was interrupted before she could say anything.

"What is that?" Uncle Jack continued, pointing past them.

Suzan and Enrique turned. On the floor of the hallway was a squirrel, well, the dismembered corpse of a squirrel, straight out of a horror movie. It lay motionless on its back, belly split open from its neck to its groin. The squirrel's ribs pulled the skin back, exposing its organs in the shape of a diamond.

Gretchen ducked her head under the table to dry heave but in a moment she jumped back, screamed, climbed up on top of her chair, and even stood on one foot to get as tall as possible. "There's . . . there's another one under the table!"

Everyone's chairs backed up at once.

Jeannie stood. "OK! OK, just hang in there. We'll fix this!"

She took the tongs from the Brussels sprouts and picked up the squirrel under the table by its foot, dragging it up and out of the room. A few people screamed again. The squirrel didn't have much blood left in it, but it did lose a tiny organ or two along the floor. Suzan went for the squirrel in the hallway. She and Enrique picked up scattered remains with their cloth napkins.

"So much death," Grandma said.

Down the hallway, in shadow, lying prone on his stomach, Henry's eyes sharpened. He knew he was dealing with an experienced hunter. A hunter who'd just defiled Henry's hard-earned trophies. The boy slunk further back into the shadows.

Jeannie saw corpse after corpse on her way to the kitchen trash. They, along with a mess of bloody paws, led straight to the open freezer door. Hanging from the freezer was a clawed-up, and now empty, black trash bag. Jeannie turned to the hallway and saw Alice staring at her from the other doorway. The cat's mouth and fur were covered in blood and squirrel hair. The end of a furry tail hung from Alice's mouth. The cat sneered at Jeannie and coughed up a small hairball.

Then she disappeared.

Jeannie returned with wet-wipes. She tossed some to Enrique and asked everyone to start eating while they cleaned up.

"What kind of person can eat without first thanking the Lord for the food they eat?" Grandma said.

"A hungry person," Uncle Jack said, and dug in.

"I'm not hungry. I'm going upstairs," Gretchen said.

Jeannie picked up a lung and started scrubbing the carpet beneath it. "No you are not, young woman. You will sit with your family."

Grandma continued her blessing where she let off earlier without skipping a beat. The table was loud, but she knew how to pray as loud and stubborn as any experienced street-side fanatic could.

"Please Lord, deliver this sinful home from the evil that lurks here. Protect your humble servant from its trappings!"

Henry carefully looked around the corner. His pupils narrowed, his nostrils flared, but his breath was slow and calm. He gently placed a squirrel heart onto the floor in front of him.

The trap baited.

A few feet from the table Enrique looked up to see if he was being watched as he scrubbed the floor with a rag. The image of him cleaning up, taken out of context, would seem very stereotypical . . . though even in context . . . he laughed.

Grandma's prayer progressed from thanking the Lord to casting blame on her fellow humans. She'd just wrapped up a well-rehearsed three minutes on the Jews and glanced over to Enrique. "At least he's making himself useful," she mumbled.

Steve woke from the TV room and joined dinner, oblivious to anything that had happened in the past quarter-hour. He stepped over Enrique. "Hey, buddy, when you're done in here, there's a ton of dishes in the TV room." He sat and plated up some food for himself.

"Steve!" Jeannie scolded.

"Eh?" Steve looked up, and then back down at his plate. "What?"

Suzan interjected. "Steve. You know Enrique. He's been here several times." She waited. Nothing. "Enrique, my fiancé?"

"Fiancé!?" Grandma reeled.

"Fiancé?!" Jeannie screamed in delight.

Suzan gasped.

She'd slipped up. "We got engaged a few days ago. We thought we'd break the news--"

"Lord help us," Grandma said and held her heart.

Gretchen found her appetite had returned and smiled, watching the reality show play out in front of her.

"Is it really illegal to marry a Mexican?" one of the younger cousins asked Grandma.

"Oh!" Steve butted in between handfuls of food. "Enrique! So sorry I didn't recognize you. How are you, bud?"

"Hi, Steve. No worries," Enrique said.

"Congrats! I didn't think that girl would ever lock somebody down," Steve said with a slice of pizza in his mouth.

"You people really do take anything you want," Grandma said to Enrique and looked at her precious Suzan. "What a shame. Suzan . . ."

"What's the matter?" a young cousin asked.

"Your Aunt Suzan thinks, like most liberals, that by marrying Mexicans and Asians and Muslims that they can somehow help them," Grandma said, "and dilute the bloodline--"

"I hate to interrupt," Enrique said, "but I'm not Mexican, I'm from El Salvador."

"Enrique doesn't need fixing. He's just fine. I love him," Suzan said over him.

Gretchen went for another roll and some more turkey. She was too distracted to taste the soap in the yams.

"Does he have a job?" Grandma asked.

"I work at the hospital," Enrique said.

"And whose job did you take there?" Grandma replied.

"I'm a nurse," Enrique said.

A couple nervous laughs from the table. Enrique smiled. He'd just finished wiping blood from the floor and decided now was a good time to take his dirty rag to the kitchen.

Suzan followed.

"I might leave," Enrique said at the kitchen sink.

"I'm so sorry, babe," Suzan said and wiped a tear away from her face. "They are the worst."

"They are!" He laughed.

More screaming interrupted them from the dining room.

"And, they've moved on!" Enrique continued.

They hurried back to the dining room.

Alice was on top of the table. She hissed at everyone in attendance, reminding them all of her owner. Alice walked towards the turkey up on the tips of her claws. Her back was arched, and she looked at the family with disgust.

Like they had been eating *her* meal.

Steve stood up, holding his bread knife, and started for the cat.

"NO!" Grandma wailed, "Just let her. Don't hurt my Alice!"

Suzan ran in. "Alice, off the table right now!"

Alice turned to Suzan and growled. *Growl?* they all wondered. *Yeah, it was absolutely a growl.*

The giant, angry, probably also racist cat took up a front paw and aimed it at Gretchen. Gretchen cowered back in her seat. Everyone else felt helpless as the cat shifted her weight, and started a swing at the poor girl . . .

BLAM!

The feline vaulted up from the table, whirled around in the air, and dropped, lifeless, to the floor.

A misty cloud of blood and fur settled onto the table where the cat, Alice, used to be.

The shot came from the hallway. Henry, in fully decked-out 1900s African safari hunting tweed, slowly emerged from the shadows. As he moved, he kept the rifle mounted up to his shoulder and pointed in the direction of the cat.

Blood coated everyone at the table, head to waist. The food was all bright red. It was a lot of blood. It was too much blood.

It was a really big cat.

Grandma wailed.

She tried again and again to stand, but couldn't get up. She ended up slinking to the floor from her chair and made a slow crawl to her precious, furry, giant feline.

Henry beat her to it. He stood over the cat and decided he wasn't a gambling man. He ended the cat with a head-shot.

Execution style.

Gretchen and the others at the table plugged their ears.

Grandma rolled on the floor in agony. "You devil!" she wheezed.

"Henry, oh my god!" his mother finally said, "How did you get that BB gun back? I told you not to use it anymore. I hid it."

"Oh, that's not a BB gun," Steve offered. "That's the .22 I bought him for Christmas."

"The what? You? When?" Jeannie stumbled.

"It was going to be a surprise." Steve smiled.

"Thanks, Dad!" Henry slung the gun over his shoulder, gave his dad a kiss, then took a black plastic bag from his pocket, stuffed Alice into it, and headed for the freezer in the kitchen. "Shoots true."

"Shoots real true," Steve answered.

The dining room was dead silent. No one moved, or breathed. Blood dripped from their hair onto the table. Blood dripped from the chandelier. Grandma passed out, or fell asleep, or did something related to being in shock.

"Someone should check that old gal's pulse," Uncle Jack mused. "See if she's still ticking."

Enrique knelt next to grandma and nodded his head as he silently counted the beats of her pulsing blood. Suzan stood next to Enrique, proud of her man.

She's smitten, Jeannie thought.

Jeannie looked at her daughter, who was sitting through her first whole family meal since grade school. And her husband, who was drunk, but at least quiet and, like Gretchen, was eating his meal without protest.

Henry called from the kitchen loud enough for Jeannie to hear, "Thanks for the hunting gear, Mom." He stuffed the cat into the corner of the packed freezer. "And thanks for the gun, Dad!"

As he walked back through the dining room, rifle slung over his shoulder, head held high and confident, Henry swung by his mom and gave her a kiss and a hug. "I love you, Mom."

Was that all she needed? She cried, just a little.

On his way upstairs, Henry gave his whole extended family a giant best-Christmas-ever smile and said:

"Merry fucking Christmas, everyone!"

Thank you to my first editor, sounding-board always encourage-r, ridiculously amazing, and super hot wife Kristy for taking care of our beautiful babies while I rewrote and rewrote and rewrote these stories. Thank you for your thoughts, wisdom, positivity and love.

I knew from the day I met you that you'd bring the best out of me.

Xavier Comas, thank you for your insane cover. I only asked for something bold and iconic that embodied the attitude of the entire book. Small order. Thank you for being there for the last step in this journey, and for bringing your vision to the cover.

Thank you to my editor Brooks Becker for getting me through the final phase of this book, your encouragement, thoughts, and the thousand adjustments that help me look literate.

Jess Deugan, your calligraphy brings so much to the details inside this book. Having it in here makes me so happy.

Kirk Anderson, thank you for your encouragement and feedback on the earliest drafts of these stories. Two hours talking story with you helped me reshape this entire book.

Thank you Mom and Dad for always supporting me and for always being on my side, I know you'll still love me after this book comes out.

Thank you to all my Cinema Geeks for your friendship and creativity. Thank you Rachel Weaver and Lighthouse. Thanks Fox•Dog Coffee, Otis Cafe, and Candlestick Coffee Roasters for keeping me awake.

Joe Movick is a filmmaker and author. He lives in Colorado with his wife and two children, where writing is equal parts therapy and personal entertainment. Christmas is his favorite holiday.

If you're interested in any other works, follow @joemovick on social media and visit joemovick.com

Made in the USA
Columbia, SC
23 November 2020